MY TWIST OF FORTUNE

PIPER RAYNE

Cover Design: By Hang Le

1st Line Editor: Joy Editing

2nd Line Editor: My Brother's Editor

Proofreader: Behind the Writer

My Twist of Fortune

Two aching hearts. One meddling small town. A second chance.

It's not a new story. Wife finds out husband's been cheating on her and she packs up her four kids and heads back to her hometown, Sunrise Bay, Alaska.

Yeah, not a fresh start, but thousands of miles away from my ex will do just fine.

I'm prepared for the cold weather, the early snowfalls, and dark days and nights. What I'm not prepared for is coming face to face with my ex's cousin and for the same feelings from twenty years ago to ignite like the flame never went out.

It doesn't take long before people are whispering about the widowed Hank Greene and me. But we both have children to think of this time around. Then again, Hank knows what it's like to be a single parent and sometimes those damn dimples of his make it hard to remember why we can't be together.

my *twist* of FORTUNE

Chapter One

Marla

I lay back on the warm sand with the sun beating down on my body. "More of that," I mumble as his dark stubbled cheek runs across my flat belly and he nestles between my legs. "I think I love you."

With a devilish smirk, he pushes my skimpy bikini bottom to the side and his sparkling blue gaze coasts up my body to meet mine. Oh, he's a bad boy all right. One swipe of his tongue and I writhe under him, my thighs opening wider. My hands fall to my sides, searching for something to clamp on to, but only sand slips through my fingers.

This man knows his way around a woman's body. I wish my ex-husband could see me now. See this gorgeous hunk of a man willingly pleasing me without the disclaimer of "I'll do you if you do me." He hooks his fingers into the sides of my bikini bottoms, staring up at me with half-lidded eyes as he lowers them down my legs and flings them behind him.

"Now where was I?" His shoulders nudge my thighs farther open.

I sigh, falling back down while the warm sun soaks my skin and the sand cocoons my body. This man is an expert. He should start a YouTube channel on how to give oral sex on a beach to a woman you don't know. He flicks his tongue and all thoughts of YouTube leave my brain because this man deserves to have every one of my nerve endings' attention. My back arches, my thighs quake, my moans deafening to my own ears.

"That's it. I'm right there. Keep going."

He presses his arm over my taut stomach. I clench to prolong the impending orgasm, but the urge to let go intensifies with every swipe of his tongue. He pushes a finger into me, quickly adding another one. I free-fall as if I'm in one of those extreme swing rides, but my harness doesn't jolt me back when the bungee cord stretches to its full capability. Instead, I fly out and soar through the sunny sky.

"Mommy?"

"Mom!"

"Is she sick?"

"She's groaning like she's gonna throw up."

"She's not groaning, she's... oh God, I'm out."

A nudge on my side jolts me, and as if a witch cast a spell, the man disappears, then the beach. The ocean is the last to fade away as I open my eyes and blink to find three pairs of curious eyes hovering over me.

I look at the ancient alarm clock with flip numbers. You know, like in the movie *Groundhog Day*? It's programmed to my dad's favorite seventies radio station so "Something's Comin' Up" by Barry Manilow sounds throughout the room as I blindly fumble to find the small button to make it stop.

I slowly rise from the bed, peeking at three of my four children. My fourteen-year-old Nikki has one arm of a shirt while my twelve-year-old Mandi has the other. The middle is so stretched out, it's a wonder the fabric hasn't ripped in half.

"Tell her she can't keep borrowing my clothes!" Nikki screeches, yanking on the fabric.

"Are you okay, Mom?" My sweet little eight-year-old, Posey, climbs over the edge of the bed and cuddles up next to me. She's my worrier and my spiritual leader, as she's decided it's her mission to find remedies to cheer me up every day.

"I'm leaving!" Jed screams from downstairs.

Nikki huffs and glares at Mandi, yanking again. "I gotta go. Give me the shirt."

I sigh and look at Posey, whose head is on my shoulder and staring up at me with her sweet smile. She runs her small hand down my arm until our hands are joined, then she squeezes because she's worried. I could kill my ex-husband, Jeff, for this. Our once-carefree seven-year-old now feels as though she has to take care of me because he decided to implode our family unit.

"Go get ready, Posey. We have to leave soon." I kiss the top of her head.

She's reluctant to let me go, but when her sisters' screams become louder and I sigh, she sees it's her best option. This room is about to shake from the volume of my yelling.

I close my eyes and swing the covers off the bed, sliding my legs over the edge to get up.

"Mom!" Nikki points.

I look down to find a giant stain on my sweatshirt from the mint chocolate chip ice cream I spilled all over myself last night while I ate it out of the carton. I stand and head into the bathroom. "Leave me alone. You two have plenty of clothes. Find something."

"No! Mom, it's mine. Tell Mandi to let go."

Jed honks the horn of the truck from the driveway. The truck that Jeff just had to buy Jed because why not buy your seventeen-year-old son's happiness with a truck instead of actually, oh, I don't know... keeping your dick out of other women's vaginas.

"Mandi, give Nikki the shirt so she can go to school. You can find something else."

"Seriously?" Mandi's shoulders sink as though I told her she has a giant zit on the tip of her nose and there's a boy at the door.

I shut the bathroom door. With my hands on the sink, my chin falls to my chest and I inhale and exhale a deep breath to find some serenity and calm. Maybe I should download one of those meditation apps or try yoga or something. All the other moms raved about it back in Arizona.

Turning on the shower, I grab the hem of my sweatshirt to strip it off, but I catch my reflection in the mirror. Oh my God. What happened to me? I'm wearing an oversized pair of flannel pants and my dad's overly large "Just the Tip" sweatshirt with a bullet and American flag on it.

"Today is a new day," I murmur.

Wheels squeal outside as Jed punches the gas pedal. I picture the back of the truck fishtailing. I'm the mother of a hoodlum. Tears prick my eyes, but I refuse to let them fall.

I strip off my sweatshirt and my pants and step into the avocado-colored porcelain tub with the valance of fabric, complete with ties and tassels. My mom does nothing that doesn't involve tassels. A rush of cold water shoots down on my back.

"SHIT!" I scream and bolt out of the bathtub, one lonely tassel tie falling to the floor.

I dry myself off before putting my sweatshirt and pants

back on for warmth then head downstairs to the kitchen, finding Mandi and Posey. Posey is dressed, backpack zipped up and a Pop-Tart and glass of milk in front of her on the table. Jesus. One day she'll be in a therapist's office, saying it all started when she was seven and her parents divorced.

"Mandi, was the water hot this morning?"

"Lukewarm." She bites a piece of toast.

"Were you the last one in?" I ask.

She eats her toast, staring at her phone. Another one of Jeff's gifts. "First."

"That doesn't make sense. Did Jed or Nikki say anything?"

She shrugs and sips her juice.

I turn on the lights at the top of the basement stairs before rushing down. At the bottom step, the sight of water on the cement floor alarms me.

"You've got to be kidding me." I tiptoe through the water and find the source—the water heater. Since it's only been two retired people living in this house for the past twenty-plus years, I'm sure it's in shock from my teenage boy, who takes three showers a day.

After running back up the stairs, I grab the home phone and dial my mom in Florida. I'd love to volunteer to pay for this since they're letting my kids and me stay in their home rent-free while they travel in their RV. Although they've offered to let us stay when they return in two months, if I want to preserve what little sanity I have left, I need to find a place of my own. Which means I need to save all the money I can.

"Hey, honey, shouldn't you be on your way to school?"

"Good morning, Mom." I ignore her question. "I think the hot water heater is done."

"Hold on." She must only move the phone a millimeter away from her mouth before she screams, "Frank!"

Posey slides off the stool and points at the clock, eyeing me to make sure I see it.

I cover the receiver. "Go wait in the car."

They actually listen, and I tap my fingers on the counter, waiting for my dad.

"I'll call Hank Greene," my mom suggests.

"No, don't do that."

Just the thought of my ex-husband's cousin coming here and seeing me makes me want to dig a hole for myself. My gaze scatters across the messy house. The carton of ice cream I finished off last night sits by the trash can. The takeout pizza boxes are precariously balanced on the counter. Jed's socks and sweatshirts litter every surface, and cups clutter the end tables. I've lost all control of my children.

I hear the phone exchange hands. "What's up, buttercup?"

"Hey, Dad, I told Mom I'm guessing the water heater is done. There's water in the basement and all I got was cold water this morning."

"Yeah, that thing has been on its last legs."

I wave my hand to get this conversation going even though he can't see me. "So who do I call? Who do you use?"

"I'm calling Hank right now," Mom yells in the background.

"Dad! Tell her no."

But I hear Mom on Dad's speakerphone. The line is ringing.

"Hank's a good guy," Dad says. "He does all the work for

us ever since his dad retired. He's the "it guy" in Sunrise Bay now."

I stop myself from saying he was the "it guy" when I was in high school too. Another reason I do not want him to bear witness to what has happened to me.

"Hey, Hank!" Mom singsongs, then her voice fades away. I strain to hear anything, but she must have left the RV with the cell phone.

"Don't you think it's a little awkward to have Jeff's cousin come and fix the water heater?"

Dad doesn't say anything for a moment. "True. Point made. Okay, well, we'll have to call someone from another town. Helen!" he yells.

I move the phone away from my ear.

Posey comes back in the door, her eyes pleading. "I can't be late again, Mom. Please."

She's right.

"Hey, Dad, I have to take the girls to school. I'll call you when I get back and we can figure it out. Give me about a half hour."

"Sure thing, buttercup."

I stuff my phone into my purse and run out the front door to my minivan. "Sorry, girls."

My tires squeal and slide as I punch the gas with the hopes my kids don't get another tardy on their record.

Little did I know my day was about to get worse.

Chapter Two

Marla

Posey already has the door open before I have a chance to fully stop the van in the elementary school drop-off.

"Pos!" I slam on my brakes and Mandi and I fall forward.

"Seriously?" Mandi says.

I roll my eyes, but it's the tapping of something on the hood of my van that causes me to look up.

"You've got to be shittin' me," I mumble, but from Mandi's huff, she heard me.

"Oh my God! Is that really you?" The blonde woman acting as traffic director beelines it from the front of the van over to my window.

"I'm going. Love you, Mom!" Posey says.

I look back to say goodbye, but the van door shuts. I watch as Posey's backpack swings right and left as she runs to the doors of the school. I move to put the van into drive, but a pearly white smile plastered to my window reminds me of the hell I'm in right now.

I press the button to lower the window.

"Mom!" Mandi screeches. "I can't be late."

Her reason for not wanting to be late isn't the same as her younger sister's, but I get it. I was a tween once too. She doesn't want all eyes on her when she walks in after the bell.

"It'll only be a minute."

She throws herself back in her seat and lets out a long annoyed sigh. "Whatever."

"I heard you were back in town, but Bill and I took a vacation together in celebration of the kids starting school, so I haven't bumped into you." Donna Demonte in the flesh. The girl who should've been voted biggest flirt senior year.

I force a smile.

Her hand reaches in and she pets my shoulder like I'm a cat. "I heard about what happened with Jeff. I'm sorry."

I nod and glance at Mandi, who's lost in her phone—or pretending to be at least. "Thanks. We're good though. Happy to be back."

She laughs. "Sunrise Bay has always been your home. I think I speak for the town when I say how happy we are to have you all here. I hear there's a football player in the family. He's going to have a challenge on his hands."

I nod before my mind actually processes what she's saying. "What?"

"Jeff was always sharing all those videos of your oldest on social media. He's a quarterback, right?"

"Um... yeah."

Jeff did always post things about Jed. But that's Jeff. He's a bragger and into one-upmanship.

"Do you know Hank's son, Cade Greene?"

She pronounces Greene as if I'm not aware of the other half of the Greene family in this town. As if Hank and I weren't in the same grade. As if we never... I shake my head from going down that particular memory lane. Then it all clicks—I forgot that Donna was Hank Greene's high school girlfriend until our senior year.

"He plays quarterback," Donna adds.

"Well, if Jed wants to play, he'll have to hope they have a position for him to fill."

She laughs. "And Jeff would be okay with that?"

"Mom!" Mandi whines.

"I really need to go, Donna. We'll have to catch up another time." I shift the van into drive.

"Definitely. Maybe we can go shopping or something." Her eyes zero in on my sweatshirt.

I finger-comb my hair as though she won't notice me doing it. "Sure." I ease off the brake. "Bye, Donna."

I drive off without waiting for her to say goodbye.

"She's a bitch," Mandi says.

"Mandi!" I scold—but how can I reprimand her when I'm thinking the same thing? The woman had it out for me in high school and I know for a fact she couldn't be happier that my marriage fell apart.

"Come on, Mom, talking about Jed and Dad?"

We drive out to Main Street and into the middle school parking lot, since the schools are minutes away from one another. The lack of cars in the drop-off lane says Mandi's going to be late. Her hand is already on the handle of the door before we come to a complete stop. Must be genetics.

"I'm sorry, Mandi. Last tardy, I promise."

Surprisingly, she nods and nothing smart comes out of her mouth. When the door shuts, I close my eyes and relish the silence. Until a honk behind me startles me and I put the van in gear, driving back to my parents' house.

The thought of Hank Greene makes my stomach flip. Although he and Jeff are cousins, they might as well have been strangers. After Jeff's side of the family moved to Arizona with us, there were no more shared holidays or occasions for all of us to get together. Jeff's dad never had a close relationship with Hank's dad. When Hank's father died, we discussed moving our side of the family back up to Sunrise Bay, but it never happened. Jeff paid for my parents to visit us so we wouldn't have to come up here, which suited them fine since it was a mini vacation of sorts with a big house, pool, and warm weather.

I've always felt as though there was unfinished business between Hank and me, although we never truly dated. After his wife, Laurie, died tragically—only a year after his dad— I wanted to reach out on the phone, but I was a chickenshit and resorted to a plant and a sympathy card from our family. For months, my mom told me how sad the town was. How everyone was on the meal exchange for the Greenes and she had arranged a babysitting routine so Hank could work.

I drive down my parents' street. They live way too remote for my liking. I love Alaska, but I'd rather live in a subdivision than on the land my parents own, without a neighbor in sight. I don't need to have a moose wish me good morning on my way to the van.

Driving up their long driveway through the forest of trees, I realize the worst part about my parents' remote location is that if someone stops by to see me, I can't just keep driving until they leave. I'm stuck.

So as my van pulls up to the house and a dark gray truck comes into view, I curse to myself. I already know who it is and my stomach sinks. I calculate my chances of pulling down the driveway and acting as though I didn't see him, but that's shot to hell when the driver's side door opens.

I say one last prayer that Hank has apprentices working

under him and it's one of them in the truck. He must have employees. I'm sure he wouldn't be too keen on seeing me either.

But just like every other facet of my life lately, this situation doesn't go my way either. Two long legs attached to work boots hit the pavement as Hank unfolds himself from the truck. He's bigger than I remember. Taller, broader. There's scruff along his face that's darker than his honey-blond hair, which is longer than I've ever seen it, as if it's weeks past a haircut but not so unruly he looks unkempt.

Just like all my friends in Arizona thought all men in Alaska looked like, he's wearing a flannel shirt, jeans, and brown work boots. He pushes his sunglasses up to rest on top of his head and offers me a wave.

I can only smile. Nausea hits my stomach as I turn off the ignition and slide out of my minivan.

"You didn't have to come," I say immediately.

He side-glances me, getting something out of his truck. "Your mom called me this morning."

"I'm sorry. I told my dad I would get someone else. I'm not even sure..."

He pulls a toolbox out of the back and looks at me. His gaze slithers across my body side to side, up and down, and when his gaze meets mine, the hazel eyes that would pierce me from across the room in high school make me want to sigh. Hank Greene.

"Hey," he says in an easy way. As if it hasn't been twenty years since we saw one another face to face.

"Hi."

He nods. "Welcome back."

I fidget with my hands and balk when I look down at my feet. I have on my mom's flowery rain boots, my dad's too-big flannel pants, and oh my God. I cross my arms over my chest. His chuckle says he wondered when I would figure out how I look.

"So the water heater... I have a key to your parents' place, but I didn't want to barge in." He changed the subject. At least I can be thankful for something right now.

"Oh, thanks. I have to warn you." I walk up the steps to the house. "We're still getting settled, so it's a little mess—"

"Marla?" his deep voice says behind me. "I have teenagers. I understand."

I whip around, guilt weighing heavily on my shoulders. "I wanted to reach out and say how sorry I was to hear about Laurie."

He nods. "Thank you."

Okay, just open the door and let him go look at the water heater. If he really wanted to have a conversation with me, he would've reached out when I first arrived in town. Not that I blame him that he didn't. If I would've had anywhere else to go after Jeff decided his side piece was the love of his life, I would've gone there. But I have no money of my own since I quit my job almost twenty years ago to raise the kids. So pathetic me now lives in my parents' house. I'm a billboard ad for why women should be independent.

"It's right in here." I open the door.

"You didn't lock the door?" he asks once we're inside.

I scramble to pick up all the dirty clothes and dishes that make it look as if we live in a frat house. "I was in a rush. I don't make it a habit to wear my dad's clothes either."

He laughs and his gaze falls over my body once again. Shivers follow the path of his vision, raising the hairs behind my neck.

He slides by me, heading to the basement. "I'll let you know what I figure out."

Then all I hear are his pounding footsteps down the

basement stairs. I fall onto the couch and wish there was some magic way it could suck me in and swallow me whole.

After a few minutes, I see that wish isn't going to be fulfilled either, so I do the best thing I can think of—get dressed in anything but what I'm wearing.

I take off the rain boots, leaving them by the door, and shed the sweatshirt on my way to the stairs, leaving me in my cami and flannel pants. As I'm passing the basement door, the footsteps grow louder and I freeze, searching for a place to hide. But unlike my eight-year-old self, I'm too big to go under a cabinet, and before I know it, Hank is standing at the top of the stairs. He stares at me, focused on my breasts straining the white fabric.

"I was just about to go change."

He nods, and his gaze bounces back up to meet mine. The smoldering look on his face is foreign to me and my body says, "Just take what you can and suffer the consequences later." I'm so desperate to have an orgasm that isn't self-induced, I'm dreaming about men. But I remind my unquenched libido that I know nothing about Hank. For all I know, he's seeing someone.

I step forward and he steps to the side, thumbing toward the front door. "You'll need a new one. I'm just going to run to Handyman Haven and pick one up."

"Oh, okay."

"I'll call your dad first."

"Okay."

We stand in awkward silence for a moment, his eyes dipping once more to my breasts. "I'll be right back."

"Okay." *Find a new word, Marla.*

He's the first one to walk away. My libido screams about what a wimp I am, but what was I going to do? Jump in his arms and kiss him?

His truck starts and I wait to hear the crunch of the gravel under his tires before I knock my head against the wall in complete and utter embarrassment. Returning home is going great so far.

Chapter Three

Hank

It takes all the strength I have to pull out of the McAlisters' driveway knowing Marla is in there —alone—wearing a tight white tank that made it clear she isn't wearing a bra. Her hard nipples were practically begging me to tear the thin material off her body and suck on them.

When Mrs. McAlister called this morning with the news about the hot water heater, I assumed that the sexual tension that had always lingered between us in high school had faded. We'd moved in two different directions. She married my cousin and me Laurie. We have families of our own, kids who are almost grown.

Rumors have run rampant in Sunrise Bay about why Marla McAlister-Greene is back in town with four kids. According to our small town gossip brigade, Jeff couldn't keep it in his pants, cheating with any woman who showed interest. They said Marla was crushed she wasn't enough for him, but she stayed for the money and security. I always assumed she stayed for the kids though. Marla was never the type who cared about money. But maybe once you have it, it changes things.

Jeff's a real estate developer, from what I know. Our dads didn't always see eye to eye, and when Jeff took Marla down to Arizona for a business opportunity he got from a college buddy, my aunt and uncle followed them. They've never returned, not even to bury my father. That's the day I lost all respect for them. I no longer consider Jeff or his parents' family, even if we share a last name. There are people here in Sunrise Bay who picked my mom up, who took care of my kids and me after Laurie passed. Those people are my family even if we don't share blood.

I park along the curb of Handyman Haven. I'll try to be in and out because downtown is like a game of gossip telephone from one store to the next. If they're not trying to fix me up, they're trying to set up my kids.

I pull my phone out of my pocket and dial Mr. McAlister.

"Hank," Mrs. McAlister answers the phone.

"Hi, Mrs. McAlister, is Mr. McAlister around?"

"How was my daughter? Did she look okay? I'm so worried. I told Frank we should head home, but he swears she's fine and a little alone time would do her good, but I'm not so sure. I mean—"

"She looks good." I refrain from telling her how Marla might have looked a little unhinged when she came out of the minivan. I've been where she is. Not exactly—my wife died—but there were days I didn't want to get out of bed. And I'm sure the kids are navigating new terrain with their dad still back in Arizona.

A long breath falls out over the phone. "Oh good. Maybe you could take her out."

"Helen, stop trying to set them up," Mr. McAlister says in the background.

"I'm not trying to set them up, but she needs friends." Her voice grows farther away until it's Frank on the phone.

"What's up, Hank? Tank is blown, I guess?"

"Yeah. Sorry, completely rusted out. I'm at Handyman Haven to grab a new one. Wanted to talk to you about how you want to handle this."

"Let me know what I owe you. I almost replaced it last year, but I figured we might as well get the last bit out of it. I guess my grandkids finished it off for me." He chuckles.

"Speaking as someone with teenagers, you're probably right."

"Helen's on my tail every day to get back up there, but this is our vacation. I feel bad for Marla, but it's not like we didn't see this all coming. Jeff's a weasel. He never deserved her in the first place."

I say nothing. As weird as it is, Mr. and Mrs. McAlister always feel open to talk to me about how horrible my cousin and his family are because of the very public feud between the two Greene brothers.

"And his dad is a whole other story. Your mother picked the right Greene there."

I nod although he can't see me. Not sure what he wants me to say. This town acts as if I don't know the story of how Ethel Mann fell in love with two brothers once upon a time.

"I'll get this new tank in and I'll clean up the mess too," I say.

"Are you sure? My grandson can help as soon as he gets home from school."

"It's a slow day for me."

"Thanks, Hank, we feel so much better knowing you're

taking care of this." He pauses before he whispers, "How is she really?"

"She's good."

"Come on. It's me. She sounds horrible on the phone." His voice is so low I struggle to hear him.

"I only saw her for about five minutes, but she's holding up." Which isn't a lie. She's standing, her kids got to school, and based on the stain on her sweatshirt, she's eating.

"Okay. Good. That's good." I can almost see his gray hair falling onto his forehead as he nods. I'm not sure my words are doing much to make him feel better.

"Well, I'm gonna head in and grab this."

"Yeah, I don't wanna take up any more of your time."

"Have fun. We'll see you in about two months, right?"

"Yeah, we're heading into the Midwest tomorrow."

"Great. Safe travels, Mr. McAlister."

"Bye, Hank."

We hang up and I climb out of my truck, rounding the back and stepping up to the sidewalk. My mind is consumed by Marla returning to town, and all those unrequited feelings swarm inside me like bees in a hive.

The bell chimes above the door. As usual, the owner, George, is behind the counter on a stool while three of his fellow members of the gossip brigade are in front of him, whispering.

"Hank!" George waves.

All three of them turn to me, waving and smiling. From the surprise in his voice, my guess is that I was the topic of conversation.

"Hey, George. Fellas." I nod in greeting. "I need a water heater."

Walking down the aisle, I locate the water heaters in the back. I know where everything is since I've been shopping here since I was in my mom's stomach. I grab a dolly and wheel it up to the front.

"Water heater, huh? I sure do hope someone's house isn't flooded?" George says.

That question is bait on the end of his line.

"Yeah, that'd really be a shame," one of the other men says.

They think they're going to trick me into saying it's for the McAlisters, then I'll be interrogated about Marla's return. Because every member of the gossip brigade are military vets, they all act as if they can pull information out of people. Sometimes I assuage them. Not today though.

"Luckily, no." I'm not lying. There isn't a ton of damage at the McAlisters', and as though Frank knew it was coming, he moved all the storage boxes up onto shelves.

"Oh, that's good," George says.

"Yeah, good," the three other men say in unison.

I pay George. "Bye, guys, don't waste too much of your day inside. It's beautiful out."

I wave and wheel out the dolly. Thankfully they didn't pressure me too hard for information. But as I load the water heater into the bed of my truck, I realize I counted my thanks way too soon—my mom and her blue-haired best friend are at my truck, their hands clasped in front of them like church ladies. Mom met Dori a couple of years ago and they've been inseparable ever since. These two are so much worse than the gossip brigade. These two make you feel like a POW.

"Mom," I say with a nod.

"Hey, Hank." She steps up to me and wraps her small arms around my stomach.

"Dori." I lean forward and kiss her on the cheek before I get the heater into the bed of my truck.

"You're so strong. I threw my back out, otherwise I could've helped you with that."

I wave off Mom's friend. "It's all good."

"Who's the water heater for? Jeez, I hope there's no water damage. I remember when ours went out." Mom looks at Dori. "And it almost ruined all of Hank's baby pictures. I was so upset, and Jim snapped at me to calm down. Let's just say I didn't talk to him for an entire week. Disrespecting me by snapping at me when it was our baby's pictures..."

Dori shakes her head in agreement. If my mom's friend wasn't here, I'd probably interrupt and say let the man rest in peace.

"Oh, but you can imagine after a week of no talking, the make-up sex," Dori says.

"It is the best." My mom laughs.

My mom looks at me. "Who's the water heater for?"

I stare blankly at them. I know my mom's game. She's going to continue this until I fess up and fill her in. But I'm going to tolerate this even if I throw up my entire breakfast on the way back to the McAlisters'.

"Let's just say Jim was all over me."

I choke on the bile rising up my throat.

"Philip used to... you know." Dori eyes me, and I'm not sure if it's because I'm positive I must be green or if she's judging if I've reached my limit yet.

Mom touches Dori's arm. "I wore this lingerie and tried to do a striptease once, but he grabbed me and tore the lace—"

"The McAlisters!" I say a little too loudly.

Hey, at least I didn't cover my ears and yell, "No, no, no make it stop."

"Oh," Mom says in that tone that speaks more than if she just said what she's thinking.

"Definitely, oh. Second-chance romance is the best." Dori smiles.

"We were never a first. She just divorced my cousin. You two better keep this between you two."

"Sure. Who would we tell?" Mom looks at Dori.

I've seen them work their magic. They think they're modern-day matchmakers.

"I'm serious. She has enough on her plate with returning to this town. She doesn't need everyone in town making up stories."

Mom stares at me in disbelief that I would think she'd spread news. "I understand."

"Do you? Because I vaguely remember you being the one to tell me about her divorce. How your voice was dripping with 'I told you so's.' She has a life and kids. Leave her be."

"You've got it bad. All protective of her. Women like that."

Dori's tone is so enthusiastic, I want to yell at her to back off. I'm confident in my skills. If I wanted to ask a woman out, I would. Well, that's a slight exaggeration. I haven't really dated since Laurie. Mostly because raising five kids hasn't left me with a ton of spare time. Chevelle's issues from losing her mom have been so ever-present, I can barely step away from her to take a piss, let alone bring another woman home.

"Listen, I'm leaving. You two need a ride somewhere?"

They both shake their heads.

"I've got my Cadi. We're heading into Lake Starlight," Dori says, making their almost identical town—minus our spectacular bay—sound glamorous.

"Yes, Dori is going to show me where she lives now. Northern Lights Retirement."

I stop walking and turn to face them. "Are you thinking about moving there?"

Mom shrugs. "The house is big, and your dad is gone. I don't know. We'll see."

Huh. I always imagined she'd live there forever.

"Have fun at the McAlisters'," Mom says, her and Dori walking down the street.

"It's not fun putting in a water heater."

"It is if you get all wet doing it," Dori yells back.

They both bend forward in a fit of laughter as if they're thirteen. It is nice to see mom laugh again though.

Maybe she should move to a retirement community, but what would she do with the house? I can't afford to buy it from her, and I know she doesn't have the cash to pay for the rent at a place like Northern Lights Retirement Center. I mean, Dori's family owns Bailey Timber Company. My dad was the best contractor in the county, but it's like comparing peas and carrots.

I glance at my watch. Shit. I better go. Just as I climb into my truck, my phone rings and I curse.

"Hello. Hank Greene speaking."

"Hi, Mr. Greene. This is Nurse Mindy. I have Chevelle in the office."

I throw the truck into drive and head to the elementary school instead of the McAlisters'. This day just keeps giving and giving.

Chapter Four

Hank

My day went from "meh" (the usual grind of getting five kids out the door), to fantastic (got to see Marla in a tight see-through cami), to annoying (picking up Chevelle from the nurse for the tenth time this month).

As I stir the chili I prepared this morning and cover up the Crock-pot, Cade pulls up in my old beat-up truck. He drops his book bag on the table, grabs a Gatorade out of the fridge, and heads toward the pantry for a snack. It's his usual routine, except instead of telling me what happened at football practice, he's quiet.

"How was practice?" I ask, breaking the layer of ice that's fallen over the kitchen.

He plops down in a chair and opens a container of Pringles. "At least they won't have to change the lineup." He puts a stack of chips in his mouth, chewing and downing them with a gulp of Gatorade.

"What are you talking about?"

"Jed Greene. His arm, Dad." He shakes his head. "It's good. I mean... I look mediocre compared to him."

"I doubt that."

He stops drinking and slams his drink down so hard, orange Gatorade spills onto the table. "I'm serious. By the end of practice, I was on the bench and Jed was throwing the passes. When Coach finally called me in, he put me at receiver."

"Well, receiver is a good position too. Remember when you said you wanted to play different positions? Maybe this is your chance."

"Not my senior year! I'm the captain of the team. I'm the one who brought this team up in the ranks since freshmen year." He jabs his finger into his chest. "The position isn't supposed to be stripped away from me my last year of play."

I run my hand over my forehead and drag it down my face. Laurie would handle this so much better than I'm about to. "Well, he is your cousin."

"Technically, second cousin." Chevelle comes in with my phone in her hand. She places it next to me. "Aunt Marla says tonight is fine."

"Tonight for what?" Cade screeches and tosses his empty Gatorade container into the trash.

Chevelle ignores her brother's outrage and leaves the room.

"Maybe basketball is more your sport," I joke, but from the look on Cade's face, he doesn't find it funny. "I have to fix her water heater and Chevelle isn't feeling well. Do you mind watching her?"

"Again? You need to take her to see someone." He stands.

I'm thankful Chevelle left the room.

"Everyone deals differently." I open the fridge and take

out the cheese and sour cream, then I spoon some chili into a bowl for him.

"It's been five years. She needs to talk to someone." He grabs the cheese and dumps more than two handfuls into the bowl before sitting back down. "You do know my life is over, right? Maybe I should be the one in therapy." He stirs his chili.

I watch for a moment, wishing I could take away his adolescent problems. "We went over this when we found out they were coming. There's more than enough room for two quarterbacks on the team."

He shakes his head and I wait for him to swallow his chili. "You know that's not true. I mean, Jeff was a quarterback, you were a quarterback, and now Jed is coming in as a senior to take the spot. It's not fair, Dad."

I slide out my chair and sit down in the one closer to him. When your kids lose a parent, especially as suddenly as they did, it's hard not to want to put them in a bubble and promise that's the worst thing that could happen in this life. And in comparison to losing your mom, not being the high school quarterback means nothing, but telling a seventeen-year-old that isn't going to get my point across.

"How about this weekend, we run some plays with you as receiver? I think you might like being the one who scores. And if Jed has the arm, maybe there's more possibility for you guys to be an even better team this year."

He nods and leans back, his hands resting at the back of his head. Sometimes I look at Cade and think I'm looking at myself at his age. He's been a mini-me since he was born. Unlike Fisher, who is all dark features like Laurie.

"I'll be back," I say. "They have no hot water heater, and from the way you smell, I can't imagine if Jed can't shower."

"Let him stink. You should see all the girls fawning over him too." Cade rolls his eyes.

I smile at his jealous tone. "Every girl? I doubt Reese was."

"I caught her staring at lunch. She said she was looking for resemblances to me, but I know better. I broke up with her."

"Cade!"

He shrugs. "She can date Jed if she thinks he's so fucking hot."

"I doubt that was it. I'm sorry you think your world is ending because of Jed, but he is your cousin. You two share the same last name. You've got to get used to this."

"No." He stands then pushes in his chair before grabbing his chili and walking into the family room.

I hear Chevelle beg him to play a game with her. To my surprise, he agrees, and she squeals in delight. Standing, I push in my own chair. Laurie picked out this table, but it's falling apart the bigger the boys get.

I call upstairs, "Hey, Adam, do you want to go with me to install a hot water heater?"

He runs down the stairs, always my eager helper. "Sure."

"Cade, you're in charge."

I walk out the back door with my eleven-year-old son and start up my new truck, staring at my old truck with Cade's football bag in the back. I understand how he feels. Hell, Jeff and I went round and round in high school too, but he was two years older than me. At least by the time I was a senior, I was the only Greene in Sunrise Bay High School.

I KNOCK on the door of the McAlisters'. It's quiet, but there's a brand new truck in the driveway that wasn't here this morning. I'm not sure whose it is. Maybe Marla isn't alone. Not that I should care.

"So I heard Xavier talking to Clara and I guess her mom said they can't have any more sleepovers," Adam says next to me.

"Why?" I peek through the windows and don't see anyone headed toward the door. I knock again.

"You know, because they're teenagers now. He's a boy and she's a girl, even if they are just friends. I think Clara's mom is worried about... you know."

"Do you know?" I look down at him with wide eyes. One super thin silver lining that came from Laurie's death is that I know my kids way better than I ever did before.

"We had the talk last year, Dad."

Now, I can be out of it sometimes, but I know for sure I never had the talk with Adam. And if his brothers beat me to it... Lord help him. "No, we didn't."

"Not you and me." He signals with his finger between us. "Me and the school. You know, where they split up the boys and the girls and talk about the girl stuff and the boners."

The front door opens, and a little girl stands there looking up at us. "Who are you?"

"I'm Hank and this is your second cousin, Adam." I thumb toward him. "What's your name?"

"Wouldn't you know that if we were related?" She slams the door and the lock clicks in place.

I glance at Adam, who's laughing. "She's sort of right. Don't you think it's weird you don't know her name? I mean, we do share blood, right?"

"You don't share blood, but you are related by blood."

"That's what I meant," he says.

I knock again and Adam presses on the doorbell. I shoot him a glare and he shrugs.

"The little girl isn't gonna let you in, so we need to wait for an adult."

A shadow comes from the house and I hear some murmurs behind the door. As it flies open, all I hear is the little girl saying, "Stranger danger."

Marla looks from her daughter on the couch back at us. "I'm so sorry. Posey is really protective."

"It's okay," I say. "Sorry about the delay earlier."

She's dressed in jeans and a long-sleeved shirt. Her hair is done and she's wearing makeup now. She's more put-together and just as beautiful. "Believe me, I understand delays."

A set of headlights pulls up the driveway and she glances around us and sighs. Could she have a date? Or someone from high school visiting her?

"Come on in," she says, stepping back and waving us in.

"Pizza!" A boy as tall as Cade, who I suspect must be Jed, slides down the stair rail. "I'm starving."

"Jed!" Marla scolds.

He stops, but I'm not sure if it's because he's listening to his mom or if he sees us. "Who are you?"

"He's supposedly our cousin or something," Posey says, crossing her legs on the couch, clicking the remote.

"Cade's dad?"

I nod.

"And your first cousin once removed, actually," Marla adds. "And you are... Adam?" She guesses correctly, which makes me the asshole who doesn't know her kids.

"I am." Adam sounds as surprised as I am.

"I'm Marla."

"Hey," Adam says.

"You'll call her Mrs. Greene," I correct.

The room falls silent.

"Like Grandma?" Adam says.

I shake my head. Damn, this is weird. Especially when I already know late tonight when I'm all alone, I'm going to be thinking of Marla and not as my cousin's ex-wife.

"Fine. You can call her Marla," I say and the tension in the room eases.

"Excuse me," the pizza guy says.

Marla's head snaps up as she grabs her wallet next to the door. "Yeah sorry."

We step farther into the house.

"I didn't want to interrupt the family reunion," the guy says.

Adam sits down next to Posey, watching whatever game show she is. Jed and I stand there awkwardly.

"I heard about practice today," I say. "Cade said you're quite the quarterback."

His smug face says he knows how good he is and he's already positive he's beat Cade out of the starting quarterback spot. I'm not usually a ra-ra guy when it comes to boosting my kid's ego. I teach my kids that you earn what you get and if Jed is better, then he deserves it, but the cockiness oozing out of this kid reminds me of his father. Unfortunately, that makes me go into "protect Cade" mode.

"Cade's been the quarterback for three years. The boys all play well together. Must be rough getting used to a new team?"

Marla shuts the door, and Jed takes the two pizza boxes from her hands. A thank you never leaves his lips.

"I guess that's the good thing about quarterback. As long as I throw the ball to them and they score, it keeps everyone happy."

I nod. "The boys are tight. Maybe Cade could take you under his wing, show you around?"

"That'd be wonderful." Marla's hand touches my arm.

Something like a bolt of electricity zings up my forearm straight to my heart, making it beat a little faster. It's been way too long since I've had a woman's touch if a hand on the forearm gets me going.

"Nah, I'm good. But thanks." Jed walks off toward the kitchen.

Marla's shoulders sink. "I'm sorry. This has been a tough transition."

I've been where she's at, when your teenage kid embarrasses you in front of another parent. "I understand." I thumb toward the truck. "I'm going to go get the water heater. Adam?"

"Coming." Adam gets up and follows me to the truck. As we're sliding the water heater out of the bed, Adam whispers, "That Jed is kind of a dick."

I want to correct my son's language, but he's got a point. The apple didn't fall too far from Jeff's tree, that's for sure.

Chapter Five

Marla

"That ego of yours needs to get checked, Jed. You're new to this school, and stealing your cousin's spot on the football team isn't something to gloat about."

"Second," he mumbles with a mouth full of pizza.

"Excuse me?"

He swallows. "Second cousin."

I go through the stacks of paperwork all the kids brought home today, annoyed, frustrated, and embarrassed by my own son.

"Can I go down and watch them work?" Posey asks, already sliding away from the table.

"Can we not have takeout tomorrow?" Nikki asks.

"Can I?" Posey asks for the second time, standing at the top of the basement stairs.

"Let me go through your stack first, then you need to ask Hank if it's okay for you to watch. But you have to stay out of the way."

She steps down one stair.

"Posey, I said wait until I go through your schoolwork."

"It's all done, with star stickers and excellent written on top. My teacher loves me." She heads down the stairs.

"Teacher's pet," Jed coughs into his hand.

I put down Posey's stack because I'm sure she's telling the truth. She's not my problem child at the moment. I pick up Jed's pile, which is mostly football stuff. Fundraiser information, the spirit wear sheet, game schedules, practices, permission slips to take the school bus, and lastly the dreaded concession stand volunteer form. I hate the concession stand, and now I don't have any of my old friends to commiserate with.

"Hey, there isn't a kid with the last name Demonte on the team, is there?" I ask Jed.

He looks at the ceiling and shakes his head. "Not that I know of, but there are some guys whose names I don't know."

Knowing my luck, Donna Demonte will be the go-to person in charge of everything to do with the football team and I'll have to interact with her on a daily basis.

I sign his bus permission slip, put the schedule on the fridge, and place the volunteer paper on top so I can pick a few dates and be done with it. In Mandi's stack, there isn't much to deal with, and I breeze right through Nikki's.

"Anyone want to talk about their day?" I take a slice of pizza.

"No."

"No."

"No."

I nod and take a bite of my pizza, thinking I'd rather go downstairs and strike up a conversation with Hank than sit here. But that would be awkward, so I sit tight.

Posey comes up the stairs. "He wants to see you," she says.

I place the piece of pizza down, wipe my hands, and head downstairs, Posey following. The first thing I see is Adam using a broom to sweep all the water toward the drain. Posey picks up another one and helps him.

"Thanks, guys." I run my hand over Posey's hair, and she moves her head out of the way as though she's too old for me to do that.

"Your parents are lucky they never finished the basement," Hank says, plugging in a light and handing it to me. "Do you mind? I was going to ask the kids but thought if it drops in the water, we might all be electrocuted."

"You don't want to leave your fate in the hands of a responsible eight-year-old?"

He laughs. I forgot how much my body responded to that sound.

"She locked me out. So she's smart too." He opens his toolbox.

I glance at the kids. Posey is asking Adam who he had for a teacher in the third grade.

"Yeah, unfortunately with all her responsibility and intelligence, she's turned into my own little mommy, worrying about me like I'm her newborn."

He glances back my way. "I am sorry to hear about you and Jeff." I raise my eyebrows, and he laughs. "He hurt you. For that, I'm sorry."

He focuses on the wrench and the nut while my throat closes up. I can tell that he's sincere.

"I bet coming back here brings up the good and the bad," he says, looking over his shoulder at me.

I glance at the kids again. Posey and Adam are each resting their weight on the brooms. Posey probably has one ear on our conversation and one ear on the conversation she's in.

I call to them, "Why don't you two go have some pizza?"

"Oh, I made chili at home. Adam will be fine."

"I have plenty."

Hank lets the topic go and the kids rush upstairs. "Seems you just signed up to be my helper."

"Is that my punishment? If so, I'll take it. Adult conversation in the quiet of my basement? All I need now is wine."

"I could have smuggled some in," he says, standing and lifting the old water heater up and out of the way.

"I could help."

"Keeps me young."

We both laugh. When you're in your early forties like us, you become very aware of how *not* young you are. I never felt as old as I did until Jeff told me he was leaving me—for a younger woman. He's so cliché.

It's impossible not to look back at my life and what I've accomplished. Or haven't. I told myself I was raising my kids and once Posey went to kindergarten, I'd enter the workforce again. But Jeff wasn't big on me working, and I hate to admit it, I was scared. Scared I wasn't qualified to do anything other than pack lunches, cut shapes out of construction paper, and drive my kids everywhere. I'm a smart woman, but I don't have anything to put on a resume to prove it.

Hank brings over a stool and swipes off any dirt on it. "Sit down. You deserve it."

"Thanks." I sit, still holding his light, and he goes back to work on the water heater. "I'm sorry about Jed. Up there. Unfortunately he has his dad's ego."

Hank doesn't say anything for a moment. "I think all seventeen-year-old boys should be cocky right before the real world drags them down a level or two." Another chuckle leaks out of him.

I sigh in relief. "True. Although I'm not sure Jeff ever got dragged down."

He stops working and looks over. "He lost you, right?"

Something flutters in my stomach. "Technically he gave me up."

"One day he'll realize how stupid he was."

"You're still as sweet as ever."

"And you're still easy to be sweet to."

All I can do is smile and hope he doesn't see the flush I feel heat up my cheeks.

I watch him work for a while, the quiet of the room a nice change from my everyday life with a house full of kids.

"Ever wake up and think how did I get here?" I ask in a soft voice. I've envisioned what my life could've been without Jeff in the picture. I'd never take away the four blessings upstairs, but what would've happened if I'd never agreed to move to Arizona? If we would've raised our kids in the same small town where we grew up?

"After Laurie's death, I'd be up late after the kids went to bed and think 'How did I become a widower in my thirties?' But usually a kid would wake up with a nightmare. I really just got Chevelle to sleep in her own bed this past year since the incident." He doesn't look as though he's on the verge of tears.

"Where did you meet her?" I never really knew Laurie since she wasn't from Sunrise Bay.

A smile comes to his lips. "She was from up north. Came here for school. We met in Psych 101."

"And that was it, huh? You two were inseparable?"

He closes his toolbox, locks it, and faces me, crouching.

"No. I wasn't ready for a long time. We were study partners, turned friends, turned more. It was a slow process."

I wonder what might have caused him to go so slow.

He shrugs and answers my thoughts. "I was kind of hung up on someone."

"Oh."

He raises his eyebrows at me, and I nod, remembering how close we became our senior year. Jeff was at college and had asked Hank to look after me. He did, but neither of us expected that feelings could develop between us. I denied them, but Hank wore them out in the open. In the end, I broke his heart by leaving for Arizona shortly after graduation.

I say nothing because sorry seems stupid. It's been over twenty years and he's had a happy marriage and a family in the time since then.

"When I found out you were returning, Laurie's reaction flickered through my mind. What would she think if she was still alive? In a small way, I think she was jealous of you."

I scoff. "As you clearly saw this morning, there's nothing to be jealous of."

He nods and stands to his full height, taking the light from my hands. The dim light coming from the bottom of the stairs becomes our only light source after he turns off the construction light.

"I should go," he says. Something in his voice makes me think it's like torture for him to be here with me.

"Okay." I struggle for breath. Having him so near feels overwhelming in this moment.

Then he steps closer. Visions of his heated gaze this morning flicker to mind and I meet him halfway. His hand touches my hip and I turn into him, my face tilting up to meet his.

He bends down and my tongue slides out to wet my lips, preparing for him to kiss me. Just as my eyes are about to fall closed, he presses his lips to my cheek.

"I'm glad you're back, Marla," he whispers before stepping back and bending to retrieve his toolbox and light.

Then he's waiting at the bottom of the stairs for me to go up first, and embarrassment floods my body that I actually thought he was going to kiss me. How stupid can I be? More than twenty years, a deceased wife, a divorce, and nine kids between us does not make for a romance.

We reach the top of the stairs and find Adam, Posey, and Mandi at the kitchen table playing Uno while Jed and Nikki are nowhere to be found.

"Would you like some pizza?" I ask.

"No, thank you. I have my chili waiting at home." He lifts his toolbox. "I'm going to put this in the truck and then grab the old water heater. Do you think Jed could help me?"

"Oh, definitely. Yeah." I walk away from him to the bottom of the stairs. "*Jed!*"

"What?" he calls down.

"Mist... Hank needs your help." I look back. "Is that okay if he calls you by your first name?"

He chuckles, glancing up from the table. "Yeah. I guess we're in uncharted territory here. I'll be right back."

Jed comes down the stairs and, surprisingly, helps Hank get the old rusty water heater out from the basement without offending anyone. Maybe because football wasn't part of the conversation. Jed really is a good kid, but his arrogance at his athletic ability is grating, even to me. It's all thanks to his father putting his only son up on a pedestal his entire life.

"Thanks, Jed," Hank says after they come back in.

"Sure thing." Jed runs up the stairs.

Since the kids are almost done with their current hand, Hank and I stand uncomfortably in the kitchen, waiting, cloaked in awkwardness.

"I see you got the concession stand volunteer form." Hank points at the papers on the fridge.

"Yeah. I'm dreading it."

He nods. "How do you think I feel? I'm the only dad who does it, and I always get stuck with Donna Sullivan."

"At least it's not Donna Demonte. I ran into her today at the drop-off."

He laughs. "She does love her whistle. But Donna Sullivan is Donna Demonte. She married—"

"Bill Sullivan?" I ask with a laugh. His smirk and nod saying we're on the same wavelength. "She married the pothead who almost didn't graduate?"

He returns my smile. "They fell in love after they returned from college. You won't even recognize him now." He taps his fingers on the paper. "I think I'm going to sign up for the first game so that I don't have to worry about the later games in the season in case they make it far this year."

I think he gives me a look like "maybe you want to as well," but I must be reading his body language wrong after downstairs. "That makes sense."

"Plus Donna never does the first home game because she's too busy with introducing the team and making banners for them to run through. She puts stakes with players names along the grass and decorates the fence. It's a whole ordeal. So if you sign up, it would save both of us from having to do it with Donna."

"That sounds like a good idea."

"Out!" Posey yells and puts her last card down on the stack in the middle.

"You're good." Adam stands and walks over to his dad's side. "I'm ready."

Hank puts his hands on Adam's shoulders, the affection between father and son obvious. "We'll leave you to your night then."

Hank turns and heads toward the front door. I rush past them and open the door. I watch them get in the truck and pull out of the driveway until his lights fade away.

"I'm taking a shower," Posey says, and she and Mandi go upstairs.

I take out my pen and look at the volunteer form. Am I asking for trouble? The pen hovers over the first home game spot. That tension is clearly still present with us and we're both single, which means there's nothing to really keep us apart. But he's technically my cousin by marriage.

Arguing starts upstairs between Posey and Nikki, Jed slams his door, then Mandi yells at him. Without second-guessing myself, I scribble my name on the first home game night. It's just so I'm not stuck with Donna. At least that's what I'm choosing to believe.

Chapter Six

Hank

The first football home game is fucking freezing. Adam, Chevelle, and Xavier sit on the bleachers to watch their brothers play. Although Fisher was called up from JV to varsity for this game, he most likely won't play. They just wanted extra players since Greywall is known for playing rough.

Donna is arranging candy bars and chip stacks beside me in the concession stand.

"I got this, Donna. You go and do whatever else you need to." *Please.*

Her hand falls to my forearm. "I don't know where Marla is, and I hate to leave you by yourself."

"I'm sure she'll be here soon. Plus, I've been doing this for three years. I can handle it."

"If you're sure?" She squeezes my forearm, or more my jacket and sweatshirt underneath.

"Promise." I slide my arm out of her hand. Sometimes I wonder if she forgets she's married.

"Okay then."

Just as Donna goes to the back door, Marla appears in the front. She's wearing spirit wear that I assume is her dad or mom's, or maybe back from when we attended Sunrise Bay High. She has on a black hat with a gold ball on top and bears embroidered along the front. She even has the mittens with bears on top.

"Where did you find all that?" I laugh, signaling for her to go to the back door.

When she walks in wearing tight jeans that show off her amazing curves and boots with a furry lining up to her calves. She looks adorable, and I want to shut the door on the concession stand and warm this place up with some body heat.

"My mom's closet. She throws away nothing." She holds up her mittens and shows me how they flip open to be fingerless gloves. "So I can handle the money."

"Awesome. I'll have to grab a pair of those."

"Don't be jealous. I'll share." She looks around, reads the labels for coffee, hot chocolate, and apple cider. "So the prices are all here?"

I nod. I can tell this isn't her first time running a concession stand. "Where are your kids?"

"They're in the bleachers, but I worry they're going to end up in here. They're still getting used to the cold."

"They can sit in here if they want."

She gives me an appreciative smile that makes her dimples deepen. "Thanks, but Posey wants to see the action."

As she says that, Donna Demonte-Sullivan's voice rings out over the speaker. "And now we welcome our Grizzly Bears. First up..."

She introduces the lineup, Cade and Jed both being

referred to as quarterback. Marla grows quiet. I'm sure she's aware that in a small town like ours, there's no need for two quarterbacks. One of them will play the majority of the games with the other only playing when we're already winning or if the other is hurt.

Cade hasn't been himself since Jed arrived. Jed's been used more in practice, and I tried to explain to Cade that Jed needs to learn the plays, the passes, what the other players excel and don't excel at. Those are all things Cade already knows from playing with this team for three years. But all he sees when he looks at Jed is his replacement.

Reese comes to the front window, all bundled up. "Hi, Mr. Greene."

"Hi, Reese. Can I get you something?"

She looks at the candy, but it's clear—since she's here without her friends—that she might not be here just for a refreshment before the game starts. Her vision strays to Marla, who is clapping for each boy being introduced, even though no one will hear her.

"This is Mrs. Greene, Jed's mom," I introduce them.

Marla sets her attention on Reese with a small wave. "Nice to meet you, Reese."

"You too, Mrs. Greene," she says and grabs a Snickers bar, leaving a dollar on the counter. "Thanks."

Marla watches Reese walk away. "Is she okay?"

"She was Cade's girlfriend until two weeks ago."

Marla's shoulders sink. "Jed?"

I shake my head. "No. Not that I know of. She was looking at Jed the first day and Cade took it as interest and broke up with her. He can be impulsive at times."

She sits on one of the stools. "Do you think it's their age?"

"I hope so. I mean, Cade's a good kid, but until Jed came here, Cade never had to deal with feeling threatened."

"I'm sorry."

"Don't apologize. It's a life lesson for him. Cade... hell, after Laurie passed, all my kids sort of became this entire town's kids. They baby them like I don't have enough love to give them. And how can I blame them?"

"Maybe they feel like a mother's love is irreplaceable."

I nod. She's right about that. Although I think I've done a pretty damn good job, they still lost their mother. "I suppose so, but I prefer the tough love approach. This is good for Cade."

"It's good for Jed too. As unmotherly as it sounds, I wouldn't mind him being dropped down a peg or two, so he understands that he won't always stand on top."

"So we won't let this thing with our kids interfere with our friendship?" I ask.

Another winning smile creases her lips. All the memories of our senior year, when I hoped she'd pick me and not go back to Jeff, resurface. How much I didn't want to cross that line, but at the same time, I did more than anything. Is it a coincidence that we're here now, both single and able to cross that line without repercussions, or is it fate?

But maybe I'm naïve to think there would be no repercussions. Would the kids understand? The town? I'm not so sure.

"Are we friends?" A blush tints her cheeks and her fingers fidget.

"We've always been friends."

Her smile widens and a rush of happiness hits me. If I were the reason for that look on her face for the rest of my days, I'd die a happy man. Can two people really pick right up where they left off after so many years and so many experiences apart from one another? As suddenly as the happiness hit me, the guilt that I'm feeling this way about someone other than Laurie weighs me down. I push both feelings to the side for now to examine later.

We run the concession stand like an art. Marla takes the orders and the money, and I fill them. The Sunrise Bay side is cheering nonstop because Jed really is one hell of a quarterback. At least it seems that way based on the five minutes I saw him play when I asked Marla if she minded if I stepped out.

Coach decided to play Cade one quarter, Jed the next, and so forth. They're two completely different players. Cade runs the plays and he's more patient, whereas Jed reads the field well, but he throws the ball away more often because of his lack of patience for the play to pan out. Cade stands on the sidelines, his shoulders stiff, his lips a straight line. It's hard to watch your kids learn a lesson, but it's better for him in the long run.

In the end, the Sunrise Bay Bears win thirty-six to twenty-two with both quarterbacks responsible for an equal amount of touchdowns.

"So are you going straight home after this?" Marla asks. "Do people still head to The Hideout?"

I laugh. "I think the kids head over to Pizza Barn now. Did you guys eat dinner? We could all go."

Her lips twist as she thinks it over.

"It's pizza, Marla."

"Yeah, you're right. Sure. Let's do it."

I do my best not to think about "doing it" with Marla, but that proves impossible.

"You know, Xavier's got quite an arm." Ned Turner clasps my shoulder as I wait for a table to clear out. "He was playing on the side of the bleachers with a few boys and it was quite impressive."

"Thanks. I guess that's the benefit of having two older brothers who play."

"Definitely, and this whole Cade versus Jed thing will turn in your favor." He winks. "I know it."

Sometimes I hate small towns. As if I'd be hung up on this and stay up at night, worrying if my son is going to play quarterback his senior year. There are so many more important things in life. "There's room for both. They're both talented."

"Oh, definitely." He leans in close, and the smell of alcohol on his breath burns my nostril hairs. I love Ned, he's our insurance guy in town, but he takes Friday night football way too seriously. "Between you and me, Cade's better."

Marla walks in with her kids, and Ned turns toward her.

"Marla Greene!" He opens his arms.

Posey grabs her mom's hand and pulls her back, not allowing her to welcome a hug from Ned. I snicker.

Marla gives him a wave. "Hi Ned. Good to see you."

"We'll have to catch up sometime. And be sure to come see me if you need insurance." He grabs his business card out of his jacket pocket and presents it to Marla as though it's a black Amex. "Call me."

She shoves it into her purse. "Sure thing. Thanks."

"I mean, I'm sure Jeff used to handle it, but—"

Marla raises her hand. "Thanks, Ned."

He takes the hint and walks away, finding someone else to talk to.

Marla does a quick round of introductions before she says, "I'm starving."

"I'm finally warming up. I couldn't feel my fingers," Mandi says.

"I see a girl from science class. Can I go over there?" Nikki asks.

"Sure," Marla tells her.

"My kids are in the game section. Want to play?" I pull some dollar bills out of my back pocket.

"You sure do know how to win a girl over," Posey says with her hand out.

"Pos, I have money." Marla digs in her purse, but I put five singles in Posey's hand and look at Mandi.

"Fine," she says, and I hand her five too.

"I'll pay you back," Marla says.

I wave her off and head to a table in the back big enough for all of us but far enough from the football team.

"Thanks." She takes off her jacket, and I'm rewarded with the sight of a sweater that's snug around her breasts. She peruses the restaurant and sits down across from me. "So is this place new?"

"Newer. Built after you guys left."

It's an old barn that was converted into a pizza place. Everyone loves it, and it's so big it easily handles a lot of people, especially on Friday nights.

"It's huge." She looks around, giving me the opportunity to really look at her without her knowing.

A waitress comes by, and after much discussion about what every kid eats, we order pizzas.

"Wine or beer?" I ask Marla.

"I'll just have beer."

"A pitcher then," I tell the waitress.

She leaves, and my eyes linger on the team table. Cade's not even socializing, and Jed is being the life of the damn party. Cade's gotta snap out of this.

Marla follows my line of vision and huffs before turning around. "I think Jeff taught him he always has to be on. Like he can't relax and just be himself. I try to tell him to tame it down a little, that people will like him for him, but you remember Jeff."

The one thing I hate about this situation is Jeff is always a topic of conversation. Will this be how it is if something were to happen between us? I have to be okay with that because he's their dad regardless.

"What are the plans between you two? Are you here permanently?"

The waitress comes over, dropping off the pitcher, and I pour our beers.

She leans back, crosses her legs, and takes a sip. "Jeff won't leave Arizona. His business is there. He tried to keep me there, but in the end, I said I couldn't do it anymore. We lived in a town where I was constantly reminded of his affairs. My friends who, let's admit it, probably weren't really my friends, looked at me with pity afterward. Other people would give me advice like 'sleep with the pool boy' or 'hire the best lawyer and hit him where it hurts.' But I just wanted to move on with my life. So I told Jeff he didn't have a choice, and since he doesn't have time to raise our kids, he eventually agreed and signed papers for me to move the kids."

"And will he come and visit?"

She shrugs. "You know Jeff. Work and money are at the top of his list of priorities." She puts up her hand. "Then probably his new girl." She lowers her hand. "Jed's here." She lowers it more. "Then the girls."

"Whoa, the girls are lower than Jed?"

She laughs. "Yep. He says it's just because he has more in common with a son, but they're not blind. I guess I'm not really sure what the future will bring or how much he'll be involved. Once Jed finishes football, I can almost see Jeff disappearing." She frowns, sadness filling her eyes.

Fuck, that's sad. Jeff's an asshole, but these are his kids. I would've followed an ex to the ends of the earth if she was taking my kids somewhere. Jeff and I might've been cut from the same cloth, but we couldn't be more different in shape.

Chapter Seven

Marla

Finally a night to myself. I left Jed and Nikki in charge of the kids, and I'm sitting at the coffee shop, The Grind, in downtown Sunrise Bay, looking up jobs. Although I get child support and alimony, I need extra income in order to move out of my parents' house. Plus, I want to show my kids that Mom can stand on her own two feet.

A knock on the window startles me, and I turn to find none other than Hank Greene's smiling face.

It's been two weeks since we've had to interact. Both football games since then were away, and we seem to be on opposite schedules, him not attending the one I went to and vice versa.

He walks in, and the barista waves as though they're familiar with one another.

"Hey." Hank takes off his Greene & Sons hat—the company he took over from his father. "Can I sit?"

I shut my laptop. "Sure."

"Want a refill?" He points at my cup.

"No, I've had enough caffeine."

"How about one to go? It's a great night. Wondered if we could go for a walk?" He sits on the edge of the chair next to me without taking off his coat.

"It's cold outside."

He laughs and nods. "True, but the coffee will keep you warm."

I playfully narrow my eyes and put up my finger. "Okay, you have once around the block."

His knuckles tap on the table and he stands before going over to the barista, who talks to him about his kids and what they're up to. She's older but not as old as us. The ease of their conversation says they know one another outside of customer and server.

Once he pays for our coffees and brings them back, I shrug on my coat, hat, scarf, and gloves. I pick up my laptop bag to swing it crosswise over my body, but Hank grabs the strap.

"We can keep that here. You can trust Zoe." He steps over and Zoe takes the bag from his hands before storing it behind the counter. He chuckles when he registers my expression. "Promise it's safe." He makes a cross over his heart.

Marla, you're not in Arizona anymore.

The bell rings as we exit. A few loose flurries fall from the sky, the streetlight making them glow.

"So how do you know Zoe?" I ask.

"Is that jealousy I hear?" His tone is playful, but he's not completely wrong.

"No. Just curious."

"I own The Grind. Well, I mean, it was Laurie's and after she died, I didn't want to sell it even though I know nothing about running a coffee shop. Zoe is the manager and handles most of the operations. Last year she invested, so she owns twenty-five percent. Eventually I'll have her buy me out."

One thing I always admired about Hank was the way he never held anything back. His life was always open for inspection and he'd answer every question honestly. It's an admirable trait.

"Why? Maybe one of your kids will want it."

He shakes his head. "Laurie and I always agreed that the kids had to make their own way. I don't want any of them to feel an obligation to take over one of our businesses or think that maybe Laurie would've wanted that for them. Does that make sense?"

"Yeah." I really admire how well Hank is raising his kids on his own. I could stand to take a lesson from him.

He sips his coffee. "So what were you doing in there?"

I groan, taking my own sip of coffee to delay the embarrassing admission that I need a job and have zero qualifications. "Looking for a job."

"What are you looking to do?"

We turn by the bay, where the shallow water is beginning to freeze. I can't see the mountains in the distance in the dark, but I know they're there. He leads us onto the walking path.

"More like what can I do? I've been a stay-at-home mom for the past eighteen years. Before then, I had limited work experience after I graduated college."

"What did you get your degree in?"

"I never graduated. Once Jeff finished, he convinced me that he had us under control and my time was best spent making a home." The weight of disappointment in myself settles on my shoulders.

"And you enjoyed that?"

"Honestly?"

He stops and nods, looking at me over the rim of his cup as he sips his coffee.

"I did. I loved raising our kids. Being room mother, going on field trips, volunteering, having playdates. Some of the best times with my kids happen when we're in the car on the way somewhere. It's where they always asked me questions and we'd have real conversations, you know? I'd never take that back, but maybe I should've had more balance. Why did I just drop all my own hopes and dreams? Sometimes I think my girls look at me and think, 'I don't want to become her.'"

His shoulder bumps mine. "You're being way too hard on yourself."

"Am I? Because I remember feeling that way about my mom at one point. I thought she didn't have any ambition. And then I turn into her. Now the man who promised he'd take care of me just threw me out and I'm dropping the kids off while wearing a stained sweatshirt and my dad's flannel pants." I find a park bench and sit.

Hank follows, his large body stretching out beside me.

"How did I get here and how on Earth do I pick myself up?" I mumble before tears sting my eyes, threatening to fall. It will be the lowest of lows for me if I lose it in front of Hank.

"Everyone has regrets, but the great thing about life is that it's never too late to change what you don't like. You can pivot and go down a different path."

I glance at him. "There's this pesky thing called qualifications that you need to get a job."

"I'm looking for an assistant. Want to apply?"

I laugh. "So I can lose a finger or two? No thanks."

"Hey now, there you go underestimating yourself. It'd probably be the whole hand."

I laugh again, and my head falls to his shoulder in a "thank you for making me not feel like a total loser here" gesture. His arm locks around my body to keep me there, then his lips press to the top of my head. He smells nice, like fresh air with a hint of fire.

I'm not sure if there's more to him offering me comfort than just being a friendly shoulder to cry on—literally—but something stirs deep in my belly.

"There are lots of options. Think about something you really love to do," he whispers. "And if all else fails, I'll hire you. But I will warn you, there's a required uniform that involves short skirts and heels."

I swat his stomach and his chest vibrates with a chuckle. I wind myself out of his hold because we're dangerously close to crossing a line I'm not sure either one of us thinks we should. Our gazes lock once there's room between us, the glow of the light above the bench shining down on his face. A face that's older and world-wearier than I last saw it in my youth, but no less handsome.

"Will you go on a date with me?" he asks before I get out the words that we're looking for trouble. His hand moves up and cradles my cheek.

I lean into his touch. "I—"

"I know what you're afraid of. The same thing you were in high school—that this town will cast you as the bad guy. The woman who went from cousin to cousin. But I don't care. I let this opportunity slip away from me once and I won't do it again. To hell with this town and their gossip and judgments."

"Easy for you to say." I slide out of his hold and stand,

tossing my coffee into the trash receptacle on the other side of the path.

"It won't be easy for either of us. I have a dead wife I loved. I grieved for her in plain sight. If we start things, I'm not naïve enough not to know what people will think."

"This town loves you."

"They'd question whether I ever truly loved Laurie. I know it, and it scares me that my kids might hear that kinda bullshit because I did truly love Laurie with every fiber of my being. I don't necessarily believe in soul mates or being fated to one person, but I do believe in listening to my gut. And my gut tells me there's still something between us worth exploring. It fucking sucks that my wife died and your husband ended up being a cheating asshole. If Laurie hadn't passed, your return would be nothing more than a friend coming back into my life. But that's not the situation. The fact is that I'm a single man and you're a single woman." He breaks the distance and both his hands cradle my cheeks, turning my face upward to look into his eyes. "I like you and I want to explore whatever this is with you. Let's start with a date. Just a date."

His hazel eyes are so earnest and endearing, there's no chance of me not agreeing.

"Yes," I whisper.

His smile could light up the Las Vegas Strip with its wattage. "Good. I'll pick you up Saturday at six."

"Okay."

We walk around the bay and back toward downtown.

"I have some stipulations about the date."

"You do, do you," I say with a smile.

"No talking about spouses. This is just for us to get reacquainted with one another."

A night where the name Jeff doesn't leave my lips. "Sounds good to me. What else?"

"No sleeping together. I'm not easy and don't want you to get the wrong idea."

I laugh and lean into him. "Well, jeez, I was planning to drop under the table and give you a blow job. I guess that's not happening now."

He holds up his hands. "I strike my last comment from the record. Maybe we can negotiate different terms."

"No way, you already laid down the law, Hank Greene. I wouldn't want to compromise your morals."

He chuckles and stops me right before we near The Grind. He presses my back to a brick wall, and I can't help but glance around to see if anyone else sees us.

"One more rule." He places his finger to my lips. "Leave it all at home. Just have a night for Marla McAlister-Greene, okay?"

It's a tall order, but I hope I can pull it off. "All right."

"You're not the best negotiator. Maybe stay away from that field of employment." He backs away and opens the door of The Grind.

I smile at Hank and walk through the door to find a member of the gossip brigade eyeing us as Zoe prepares his coffee. His eyes zero in between us, presumably to see if we're holding hands.

"They're still around, huh?"

Hank catches his eye. "Hey, Earl."

The guy nods his hello.

Hank leans in close to me. "Alive and kicking. They're on to us, just so you know. This will be reported to the others and a full investigation might be launched."

I laugh as Hank reaches over the counter to retrieve my

bag, then he secures it over my shoulder. "I forgot what a gentleman you were."

"I forgot how great it feels to have someone to be a gentleman with."

Warmth fills my veins, and as though I have the power to see the future, a feeling comes over me that I've never felt before, not even with Jeff. As though I'm right where I should be. As though I was meant to be in this moment at this time in my life. A serenity calms my anxiety for the first time since I've been back.

He puts his arm out as an offering. "Now let me see you home."

I slide my arm through. "Well, thank you, sir."

We leave The Grind, and as the snow spins through the air, falling to the ground, I find myself falling too.

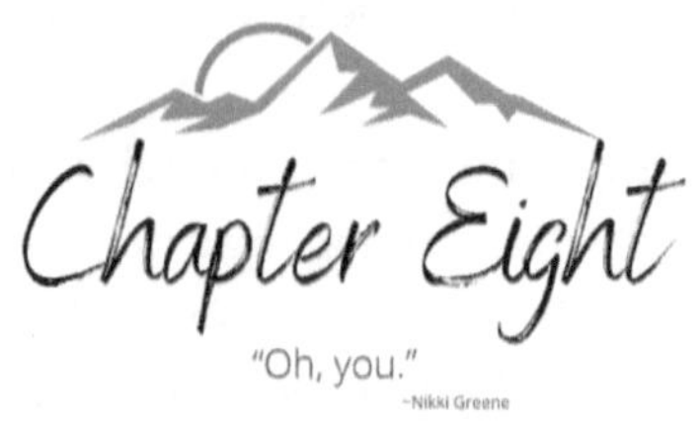

Chapter Eight

Hank

"You can't go out with her," Cade says. "She's your cousin."

I button up my shirt. "No, she married my cousin. And they're divorced, so she's not related to us anymore."

"Dad! Are you trying to make us outcasts?" Cade stands in the doorway, watching me. He didn't play last night as quarterback. Instead the coach tried him out as tight end.

"You're not going to be outcasts. You've all lived here your entire lives."

"The guys are gonna razz me about kissing cousins or some crap like that. Hell, Xavier is already getting it because he hangs out with Mandi now. People are saying they'll have babies with three heads."

"Are you telling me Xavier wants to date Mandi?" I grab my wallet and keys.

"No. Gross. Are you listening to me?" Cade puts his arms on either side of my bedroom door as though he's going to stop me. "It's bad enough people are all high-fiving Jed now and he's got all the girls' attention at school. This is only gonna make it worse for me."

"You'll play the next game. Stop worrying." I wait for him to get out of my way.

"Dad, you can't leave." Chevelle winds through her brother's legs and secures herself to my legs, holding tight.

"Cade is going to watch you tonight. He said you get your game of choice." I look at Cade with pleading eyes.

He sighs and nods. Mostly because Chevelle loves to play card games and she's kind of a card shark who never gets enough. God help me if she ever discovers poker and plays for real money.

"Really?" She looks at Cade.

He sighs. "Adam was looking for you," he lies and we both know it.

"What does he want?" she asks.

"He said he can beat you at rummy. Go school him." Cade steps out of the way.

Chevelle runs out, me following before Cade can cage me in again.

"Dad, please, think about how this is going to affect me." He follows me down the stairs.

I grab my jacket from the front hallway closet. "Believe me, no one will even know we went on a date. I'm taking her to Anchorage."

That relaxes his shoulders a bit.

"But I'm gonna be honest with you," I say.

Adam runs down with Chevelle right behind him. "I never said that. Stop following me. Dad!"

"I like her. I asked her on a date because I want to get to know her again. So you might want to start getting used to the idea that I might have a..." I pause when the word girlfriend comes to mind. It makes us sound young and inexperienced.

"A what, Dad?" Chevelle asks.

Adam stares at me too.

"A new mom." Cade looks at his sister. "Aunt Marla is going to be your new mother."

He rushes up the stairs while Chevelle's mouth falls open. "Who will be my mom? I don't want a new mom." She kicks me in the shin and follows her brother.

"I like her. She seems nice," Adam says with a shrug and heads into the kitchen.

I take a deep breath before leaving the house. I'll need to talk to the kids about me dating. Because although I've been alone for the five years since Laurie passed away, it's time that I get back out there, whether it's Marla or not. They need to get used to the idea that I might have someone special in my life.

"Cade, you're responsible!" A door slams and I escape the house into the quietness of my truck.

On the way to Marla's, I can't help feeling as though I'm biting off more than I can chew. Maybe Cade's right. Maybe my time to make something happen with Marla has passed. I can't resurrect the us from high school. Maybe those two vines weren't ever meant to wrap around one another and become one.

If only I could stop the gut feeling that says this is right and our time is now. It's what I trusted when I asked Laurie to marry me. I trusted that gut feeling after she died, and again when I took over my dad's business. It can't be steering me wrong now.

Pulling into Marla's driveway, I find Posey sitting on the stairs up to their front door. I park and climb out of the truck. "Hey, Posey."

She pats the spot next to her, so I sit, holding back my smile. "Mom says you two are going to dinner?"

I nod. "Yeah, we are."

"Without any kids." Her small eyebrows rise up into her hairline.

"Sometimes adults need adult time."

"Uh-huh. My daddy used to take my mom on date nights. Is that what this is?"

How come I think Jeff only did it when he did something wrong or felt guilty for sleeping with someone else? "It is."

"You like my mommy?" She turns to me and crosses her arms.

"I do."

She nods as if that pleases her. "She smiles a lot around you."

"I'm glad. I smile a lot around her too."

She narrows her eyes ever so slightly. "I think she likes you."

"Even better."

She stands and steps up one stair so she's eye level with me. Her long red hair is half pulled back with a few pieces escaping. Her finger juts out as she points at me. "You better not hurt her."

I hold up my hands. "I promise."

"My daddy hurt her."

I frown. "I know."

"Okay." She rushes up the steps and opens up the door. "Now you ring the doorbell so we can answer, and you can wait for her to make her entrance."

Before she has a chance to shut the door, I put up my finger. "How old are you again?"

"Age is just a number," she says, points at the doorbell, and closes the door quietly.

At least one of Marla's kids isn't going to give her trouble.

I ring the doorbell, and no one answers. Through the side window, I see Posey on the couch six feet away. I ring again and the blonde daughter, Nikki, answers the door.

"Can you not hear that?" she says to Posey on the couch. "Oh. You." She leaves the door open and walks away. "She's still getting ready."

"Thanks."

Nikki leaves the room, blowing on her nails, and Jed walks in through the back door, a sweaty mess.

He nods to me. "What's up?"

"You working out?"

Two more large bodies follow him. Derek and Lincoln from the football team. Guys who are usually found hanging around my place. I blow out a breath.

"Mr. Greene!" Derek says, putting up his hand for a high five.

"Derek. Lincoln." I nod at them both and give Derek the high five he's looking for.

"Jed's got a killer gym in the garage out back. Better than the school's. We were just working out." Lincoln thumbs in the direction of outside.

"Nice. Hope it will help. You boys really needed a win yesterday." I mentally reprimand myself for resorting to adolescent passive-aggressive bullshit because Jed was the quarterback at last night's game when they lost.

Although the loss wasn't completely his fault, he helped it by throwing two interceptions, one that resulted in a pick six. But I'm the grown-up here and need to act like one.

"We still have state in the bag," Jed says.

I nod, biting my tongue.

"Next week we play Lake Starlight!" Derek rubs his hands together. "I can't wait to crush them."

"Let's just be happy they don't have Liam Kelly anymore," Lincoln says.

"Truth," Derek says.

Jed can't bring much to the conversation since he's new to town. I'm about to fill him in about Liam Kelly when Marla comes into the room. She's wearing dark pants, high boots, a short black sweater, and a coat swung over her arm. She's gorgeous. Especially with her chestnut hair down and curled.

"Hey," I say, standing.

The three boys stand there looking from Marla to me.

"You're going out with Jed's mom?" Lincoln asks with wide eyes.

Shit. I guess my date with Marla won't be as on the down-low as I'd hoped. *Sorry, Cade.*

I ignore them and break the distance to her. "Ready?"

"Yeah." She takes the lead, grabbing her purse from by the door. "Nikki is in charge, okay?"

Jed is still speechless. I guess Marla didn't tell him about the date. She hugs Posey, then we're outside with three teenage boys gawking at us through the living room window.

"I've never been able to get a room full of teenage boys not to say a word." I open the truck door and she climbs in as though she's used to pick-up trucks and not fancy sports cars that take corners on a dime.

"I didn't tell Jed. He mentioned going out, so I thought he'd already be gone. Or out in the garage. I wanted to just enjoy this evening and save having to listen to his thoughts about it until after our date."

I round the front of the truck and slide in beside her. My keys hover by the ignition. "You look stunning, by the way. I might have to rethink my stance of not sleeping with anyone on the first date."

She laughs so hard, her head falls back to the headrest. "Sorry, I've been repeating the rules to myself all week so I don't break any."

I start the truck. "Let's get out of Sunrise Bay and head somewhere we aren't considered cousins."

"Sounds great to me."

On the drive, we make conversation, mostly about the weather and football. Easy topics.

I park in the lot of the cooking school. "I couldn't stand the idea of us in a stuffy restaurant or watching a movie. This place has a cook-off. Couples each make a meal and the owner judges."

She giggles. "And what do we win?"

"I think a coupon to come back. It's more about the experience."

She nods. "Awesome. Let's go win a coupon."

Her hand goes for the door, but I stop her with my hand on her arm closest to me. "Hold on."

I climb out of my truck and head to her side, where I open the passenger door and offer my hand. The softness of her palm spurs me to think of what it would feel like to have it wrapped around another part of my body. I feel like a thirteen-year-old again, not a man in his early forties. Jesus.

We walk into the cooking school hand in hand, and we're the youngest couple by probably twenty years.

"I think we've got some ringers here," I whisper.

"Might as well forget the coupon." She glances at her watch. "Isn't it past their bedtime?"

We share a laugh that disrupts the other couples, and all their eyes land on us. Marla slides to my side, almost hiding behind me.

"Hank and Marla, right?" Kat, the woman in charge, asks. I talked to her on the phone about getting a spot for tonight. It's been a while since I've done anything like this.

"That's us," I say. As weird as it might be, I love referring to Marla and myself as us.

"Great, let's get some aprons on you both and get started. The menu is at your station." She hands us two aprons.

I tie Marla's in the back, and she ties mine. We wash our hands and listen to Kat go through the directions. When she finishes, I'm put in charge of cutting vegetables.

"Do you cook a lot?" I ask Marla as she puts together a marinade.

"I cooked, but I'm not a cook. I'd always try these elaborate recipes"—she whisks away—"and we'd end up throwing most of it out."

"When L—"

She points at me.

I laugh because I almost mentioned Laurie's name. "I live and die by the Crock-Pot."

"I never was prepared enough. I'm a 'go to the grocery store an hour before I have to cook' kind of person."

"Mom brings things over sometimes, but she's got this new friend now, so I don't see her as much as I used to."

She puts the meat in the marinade, washes her hands, then puts a plastic wrap over the dish and places it in the fridge. "How is your mom?"

"She's fine, and if you run into her, I'm sure she'll be bragging about me. I've already gotten the third degree from her about your return."

"What can I say? Mothers love me. Well, that's not completely true."

"J—" I laugh as I almost mess up again by saying her ex-husband's name.

"I'm thinking we should've made up some penalties if you mess up." She leans forward, taunting me.

If she was mine right now, I'd kiss her because she's adorable when she's playful.

"What would the penalty have been?"

"Hmm..."

She's thinking about it, but Kat interrupts us before Marla can answer. She gives us directions on the next step.

"I'm not sure why I didn't think of this before, but we might just win this thing with my salad dressing recipe." Marla heads to the food area to grab lettuce for a salad.

I continue chopping and wait for her to explain when she returns. I haven't had this much fun since... well, I need to keep my own promise. As hard as it is, if I really want to move on, I need to push Laurie out of my mind, at least for tonight.

Chapter Nine

Marla

How did I not think about this when Hank mentioned the cooking school? I grab vinegar, oil, and all the spices and herbs I'll need.

When I return, Hank is chopping the lettuce. "Tell me about this salad dressing that will secure our victory."

I glance around and pretend as though someone might be able to hear us and steal my recipe. "About two years ago, I went on this diet, and all the low-calorie salad dressings were awful. So I did some research and started making my own. The diet wore off, as they always do."

"They always do," Hank says with a chuckle.

"But I continued to use them because at least they cut calories still and they tasted really good."

He places the lettuce into a bowl. "I can't wait to taste it."

With that declaration, nerves consume me. Jeff liked my salad dressings and that's saying something, but my mother-in-law always said they tasted homemade. I wanted to pull my hair out and say, "Because they are!" I mix the ingredients together and set the bowl in the fridge because I need it to chill as long as possible for the flavors to come out. At least the herbs are fresh, which will help the flavor come out faster.

Hank and I work side by side. He tells me about his dad and taking over the contracting business. I try to steer clear of talking about the kids because that leads to talking about Jeff. I can't help but feel boring because unless he wants to know how to make homemade Play-Doh, I don't have much else.

"Do you feel like Sunrise Bay has changed at all?" he asks.

"A little bit. I mean, it's taken on a very different look. More modern."

He nods. "You should come to the town meeting next week. They're talking about tearing down the old fishing wharf because Art Billings died last year. Before he died, the place was getting pretty run down, but no one has maintained it since he passed. My son's friend's dad wants to buy it and build it into a tourist attraction with boats that go out on the water. Then the fishing boats could use it too."

"Art Billings died?" He was a good man. He had no family to pass his company down to and I'd always hoped he'd find someone he trusted enough to sell it to, but I guess he didn't.

"Yeah, his health had been declining for years. But the whole town is torn on the issue. Cameron—that's my son's friend—his dad is really pushing hard though. I think we can all agree that an increase in tourism comes with both the good and the bad."

"That's true. You think of the money it can generate for the town's businesses, but I'm sure our small-town feel will suffer at the same time."

"That's why you should vote. You are a resident again."

"Technically, I'm not. I'm living with my parents."

"Did you change your license to an Alaskan one?"

"Yes."

"Then you are. Come on. We'll go together. Really get this town talking." He winks.

"I'll go, but maybe we shouldn't walk in together. We could pretend both of us being there is a coincidence."

He smirks and shakes his head, placing the meat on the small griddle we were given. I can't tell if he's happy or disappointed. "Deal."

Kat tells us all that we have fifteen minutes until we have to present our meal. I can't believe how fast time flew by. I run to the fridge and grab our salad and dressing. Hank prepares the vegetables and the meat while I do the salad, waiting until only a minute until the bell goes off before I put the dressing on, so it doesn't make the lettuce soggy.

The buzzer goes off, and Hank grabs me and wraps me up in a hug.

"Great job, partner," he says in my ear.

"Thanks." I'm taken aback by his show of affection, but the longer I remain in his arms, the more I realize that I feel safe. Being this close to him makes me happy.

The entire time we were preparing the meal, I kept wishing I could kiss him. I wonder how he kisses, if he'll be slow or urgent. Will the tension release and we'll claw at one another until we're satisfied, or will we be slow and savor each other?

After we separate, Kat comes by and tastes our food. She takes a bite of the salad and points. "Love this dressing."

I smile wide at her. "Thanks."

"You went out on your own, huh?"

"I did."

Hank sidles up next to me, his hand resting on my hip as though we're a real couple. One who will be going home and sharing a bed tonight.

"And my guess is this strong guy cooked the steak?"

"I did," Hank says, and his hand squeezes my side.

I find myself sinking into his solid weight. The physical nature of his job has made sure those muscles he used to have under his T-shirts in high school are still there.

"Nice. You two did great." Kat sounds surprised, as though she thought we were failures from the minute we walked in.

As she goes to the next table, Hank takes a fork and stabs the salad. He chews and swallows, eyes widening. "Damn, that's good, and I'm not a salad guy."

"Not a lot of Alaskans are."

He mocks offense. "Don't stereotype your new home."

"I'm just saying." I shrug with a smile. Jeez, I can't seem to stop smiling around him.

He points at the salad with his fork before stabbing another forkful. "This is what you should be doing."

"What?"

"Make salad dressings and sell them."

I laugh. "You're insane."

He continues to eat the salad, and I pick up a fork to eat it as well. It is good, but how would I ever start anything like that? There have got to be so many rules and regulations with food.

"I see your mind whirling at the possibilities," he says softly. Then he takes the bowl of lettuce with the tongs and stops at the first table beside us. "Try this and tell us your opinion."

They look at him skeptically, but they taste it and smile and nod as though they're in agreement.

Hank goes around the room, and my cheeks heat the more praise I get. It wasn't even chilled long enough.

He returns with an empty bowl. "Now I'm going to need you to whip up a batch for my own private use. The doctor said I need more greens." He pats his flat stomach.

A weird rush comes over me, and it takes me a minute to realize what it is. No one except maybe my parents have ever believed in me like this. I step up to him and rise on my tiptoes, my lips pressing to his.

At first he freezes and doesn't move. I shift to fall back on my heels, but his arm swings around my waist and he keeps me plastered to his body. His tongue slides in and I melt into his hold when it glides against mine. Forgetting where we are, I moan into his mouth and he groans, his hand falling to the back of my head.

Clapping commences around us. I tear my lips from his, turning my head to look away from everyone and pressing my cheek to Hank's chest.

"Sorry, folks, we're new to this dating thing." Hank puts up one hand.

Someone in the room refers to young love. I giggle because we almost have adult children.

"Never let the romance die," one man says.

"Gotta keep that sexual energy alive and kicking," a woman says.

As more comments roll around, I grip Hank to shield me from my embarrassment. He doesn't seem to mind, wrapping his arms around me. I forgot how nice it felt to be part of a couple.

THE NEXT FRIDAY, I'm in the bleachers with a blanket over my lap and Posey at my side. Mandi and Nikki claim their blood hasn't thickened enough yet, and since it's only growing colder, they opted to stay home. We're playing Lake Starlight High School, who I guess Sunrise Bay beat last year at state. It's a big deal and is all Jed talked about this week.

"Go, Jed!" Posey screams, although there's no way he heard her over the cheerleaders on the track.

"Hank!" someone in the crowd says.

My gaze can't help but seek him out. He's at the fence, talking to whoever must have called to him. His youngest, Chevelle, is at his side. Adam and Xavier are throwing a football back and forth behind him.

Other than us meeting again at The Grind on Wednesday, I haven't seen him. But he did text me and ask if I wanted to do pizza tonight again after the game. Another night with just the two of us would be nice but it's not to be. With my parents not being here, I have no babysitter.

Hank shakes the guy's hand and looks up in the stands. I try to act as though I don't care, a game I would have played in high school. Good thing Posey wasn't my wing-woman back then.

"Hank! Hank!" Posey raises her hand.

He smiles and walks to the set of stairs closest to us. My stomach feels as though there's a little girl jumping on a trampoline in there. Every time he gets stopped by someone on his way to us, I want to scream.

After what feels like a lifetime, he's at the edge of our bleacher. "May I?"

Posey slides over and I slide too, leaving enough room for him and Chevelle. Chevelle pulls coloring pages and markers out of her backpack.

She looks past me and her dad at Posey. "Do you want to color?"

"Sure." Posey throws the blanket off her lap, and the two girls go farther down the bleacher to spread out more.

"How was your week?" Hank asks, his knuckles running along the side of my thigh where no one will see.

"It was okay. My kids are officially done with salad and dressings."

Ever since we went to the cooking showdown, I've been trying to master the recipes, replicate them, and figure out a way to do something more with them.

"Bring them to my place. Though my boys are kind of meat-and-potato guys. Chevelle loves salad though."

I smile at him. "I'll bring some over this week."

"Great." Hank winks.

There goes my stomach again. "Did you want some blanket?"

"Hey now, I'm a man. I don't need a blanket." He chuckles but takes the edge and slides it over his lap.

A huge roar erupts in the crowd, but I missed the play.

Hank leans toward me. "There are more pluses to having a blanket over you other than warmth." His large hand covers my thigh under the thick material.

I swear I might pass out from the exhilaration of having his hand on me. Has it really been so long since I've felt sexual arousal that a hand on my thigh threatens to send me over the edge? I lick my lips and find him staring at them.

One of Chevelle's friends comes over and asks if she wants to go play with the other kids down where Adam and Xavier are.

"Sure." Chevelle stands.

Posey stares at her coloring page, looking sad.

Chevelle stops after a couple of stairs. "Aren't you coming?"

Posey's face lights up and she looks at me for permission.

"Just stay with Chevelle, okay?"

"Okay." Posey scrambles to her feet, almost tripping, and leaves side by side with Chevelle and her friend.

"That was nice," I say.

He squeezes my thigh. "Want to go grab some hot chocolate?"

"Aren't we supposed to watch our kids?"

His hand falls in mine and he tugs. "Come on. How often are all of our kids distracted?"

He's so right. We don't hold hands as we walk down the bleacher stairs, but his knuckles brush mine more than once. There's something to be said about trying to remain a secret.

He buys me a hot chocolate then nods toward the rear of the bleachers. "I know a short cut," he says with a devilish smile.

"You do, huh?" I follow him.

I'm not surprised there's no shortcut behind the equipment shed, but there's a secret little place no one can see. He takes my hot chocolate and puts it on the ground beside his.

"You think just because you got me behind a shed I'm going to make out with you?" I feign indignation.

He moves in front of me and backs me up until my back hits the woodshed, his fingers weaving through my hair. "I'm resorting to horny seventeen-year-old tactics because there is no way I was going to go that entire game without kissing you."

"I don't remember being asked."

His lips stop right before touching mine. "Make my year and allow me to kiss you, Marla?"

I nod, and he tentatively places his lips to mine. The minute his tongue glides along the seam, it's game over. I wrap my legs around his waist, and he presses me back firmer. He feels so good. My body alive and demanding more. He nips at my bottom lip and I pant as his mouth lowers, his thumb running down the front of my throat.

"Fuck, this is trouble." His voice is gravelly, and my core clenches.

"I know." I pant for a breath because my body went into inferno territory from one kiss.

Two kids holding hands walk around the shed and startle when they see us. We break apart and they scurry off.

"I guess this is a popular place," I say.

He kisses me one more time without tongue. "Go out with me again?"

Did he really think it was a question I would say no to?

"Only if you promise to kiss me like that again."

His deep chuckle promises to send me to the edge of my sanity with need. I can't wait.

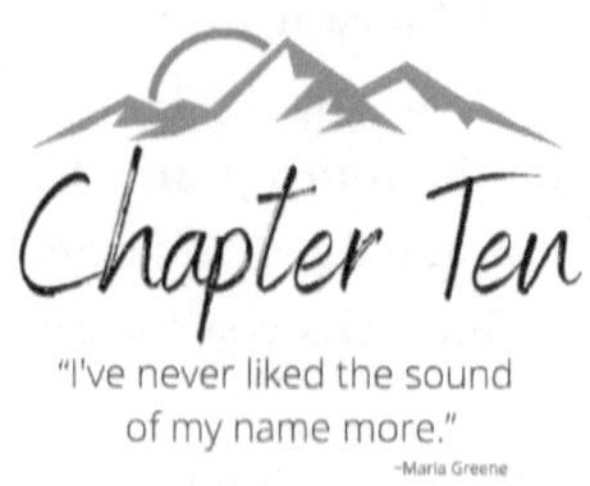

Chapter Ten

Marla

We pull up to Glacier Point Resort in Lake Starlight and my stomach grows giddy over having an entire night alone with Hank. Part of me feels as though our relationship is skyrocketing into space with the speed of a space shuttle, and another part of me feels as though we've been together forever.

For the past month, we've met at The Grind on Monday nights. We're not affectionate in public, and since he owns the place, it's not uncommon to find him there. I think that helps with the gossip. Hank comes to dinner at our house on Tuesdays, though Jed always says he has to work out. I go to his house with Posey and Mandi on Thursdays, where Cade hardly looks me in the eye. Hank surprised me after the last football game, telling me his mom would watch all the kids at her house for the night. Jed and Cade opted to stay on their own at their respective houses though. I've yet to talk to Hank about my concerns for those two.

A valet opens the passenger door of the truck, and I step

out and wait for Hank to join me. We walk through the rotating doors and find the lobby packed with people.

"I'm going to check-in." Hank kisses my cheek and walks over to the reception area.

I take in my surroundings. The chandeliers, the bustle of life with laughter and smiles and cheer. Everyone looks as though they're having the time of their lives. I kind of feel that way too. I let my vision linger on Hank, who's looking right at me. We share a smile. It's been so long since I remember feeling so hopeful about my future.

After Jeff left, I imagined my life would be put on hold until the kids all grew up. What man would want a woman raising four children? But with Hank, I can't help but think... maybe. Marrying a man like Hank would be so different from my first marriage. Better for sure.

"Ready?" he asks, coming back to me. His hand slides into mine. "They're bringing our luggage to our room."

"Great."

We take the elevators up to the fourth floor and walk down the empty hallway to our room. I think we're both unsure how this will go. Other than kissing and some feeling-over-the-clothes make-out sessions, we haven't done much about the sexual part of our relationship.

He opens the door and I step into a lavish room with a perfect view of the mountains and a lake so clear I could probably see straight down to the bottom. I sense him drawing closer to me before his arms wrap around my waist and he tugs me back to his chest. "There's no pressure."

I circle in his arms to face him. "I want to. I want this."

He bends his chin down and kisses me. "Me too."

"But..."

He chuckles. "We're both rusty." He kisses me again.

A knock on the door interrupts us. Hank welcomes the

bellboy in, tips him, then shuts and locks the door behind him. I sit on the edge of the bed with my palms on either side of my legs.

He stares at me until I look at him. "You need to relax."

"It's been a while. Like even before I divorced."

We've never really talked about whether Hank has slept with anyone since Laurie passed away, and I don't want to ask outright. Rusty could mean two months by some people's perspective.

"Do you want me to do a striptease?" His fingers go to the buttons on his shirt, and he wiggles his hips from side to side as he unbuttons it. He takes it off, leaving him in a T-shirt and jeans.

I laugh, but he continues sauntering my way, teasing me as he raises the hem of his T-shirt and lowers it back down. His hands slide between my inner thighs and he steps between my parted legs.

"If it makes you feel better, you're my first after Laurie."

My heart trips over a few beats. "Really?"

He shrugs. "I never liked anyone enough to put myself in a sticky situation. You do know the only way not to get pregnant is abstinence." He uses a teacher tone.

I giggle. "Are you suggesting you're okay if I get pregnant?"

"I like you enough not to care about any repercussions. I just want in your pants."

"Can you be serious for a minute?"

He leans into me until my back hits the mattress and he's hovering over me. "Can I kiss you?"

I swat his chest. "You know you don't have to ask me that."

His lips meet mine and I slide my arms around his neck. The weight of his body falls over mine and we both slide to get higher up on the bed. His thigh nudges my legs apart and he grinds into my core. I move my arms to reach under his T-shirt, but he grabs it by the back and tugs it over his neck, leaving his chest exposed for my viewing pleasure.

Forget milk, contractor work does a body good. Damn, he's all rippled and smooth and flat.

"I love your body," he says, his hand sliding up my sweater.

Nudging him off me, I get up on my knees. He lies down on his back, his fingers unbuttoning my jeans. He lowers my zipper, getting a glimpse of my panties. It's hard to find a place to have a wax job without everyone knowing it, so I drove all the way to Anchorage in preparation for tonight. I pull off my sweater, leaving me in my white cami, sans bra.

"Stay right there, I'm getting some water to put out this fire." He pretends to shift to get off the bed, but rises to his knees and kisses me, his hands molding to my breasts, tugging the fabric down so my breasts are exposed.

When he leans back to appraise his work, his eyes smolder and all that worrying I've been doing about this moment dissipates. This man wants me and feeling wanton is the biggest aphrodisiac there is.

He takes my legs out from under me and my back falls to the mattress only seconds before his mouth covers my nipple and sucks it. My fingers wind through the strands of his dark blond hair while my eyes fight to stay open despite the sensations rushing through my body.

I'm not sure I remember Jeff ever cherishing my body like Hank is. His mouth never stays in one place too long, as though he's worried he'll leave a part of my body untouched. I welcome the exploration because I fully intend on exploring his body over the next twelve hours too.

Somewhere between the kisses and touching and moaning, we shed each other's clothes. I watch Hank get off the bed, heading to his overnight bag, and I'd like some of whatever he's doing. His body is amazing for being in his forties, and his long thick length pointing north makes me tingle with just the thought of him inside me.

"What?" he asks, standing at the foot of the bed, rolling on a condom. "I figured better safe than sorry."

I rise up on my elbows. "I have an IUD."

"So off?"

"Are you clean?" I can't stop the smile spreading across my face. I'm barely able to swallow my laugh. We both know we're clean. The first thing I did after Jeff told he'd been cheating was get tested. Not like we had been sleeping together anyway.

He tears it off and tosses it into the trash can. "Bareback it is."

I open my legs wider, welcoming his hips. The tip of his dick pushes against my opening.

"You're sure?" he asks.

I nod. "Kiss me."

He does, and his tongue licks the seam of my lips as his hard length slowly enters me. At first we're all sensual movements, gliding, sliding like trained ballet dancers. But after he's fully inside me, he stills and I lock my legs around his waist. After a few seconds, he moves, but his head dips to take my nipple into his mouth and his hands grab my ass.

He thrusts instead of gliding into me. It's incredible how fast he gets me right to the brink of my orgasm. I'm clenching my walls around him so hard to keep from coming that Hank is growling. I've never been so happy I practiced Kegel exercises after my babies.

Soon though, I lose all control and my hands can't get enough of him. Words of praise drip from my mouth about how good he is, how I've never been this turned on, how badly I want to come. His only answer is to tell me how much he loves fucking me and how he's dreamed of this moment since I arrived back in town. Sweat drips between our bodies and Hank looks down at me with so much emotion in his eyes, my orgasm waves the white flag. I come so hard, every muscle in my body tenses so that I'm gripping him like a fist.

A devilish smirk crosses Hank's face and he relentlessly pumps into me before a few off-tempo thrusts and a loud groan. He falls on me, kissing me before rolling over and lying next to me. Shit, I've been missing that in my life for a long, long time.

"I'll be right back," he says, still panting.

He comes back with a washcloth, and after we're both cleaned up, he opens the sheets and comforter for me to slip under.

"I think we deserve an afternoon nap," he says.

I nuzzle into his chest, his fingers running along my back, and that same sensation wraps around me. That I'm exactly where I'm supposed to be.

THREE HOURS LATER, I wake up to the door clicking shut and I bolt up, finding the bed empty. I look around.

Hank is wheeling in a room service tray. "Did you think I left you?" He chuckles. "I'm waiting for the encore."

Did I? No. I think I was just in such a deep sleep, I forgot where I was. I turn toward the clock, happy to see I didn't sleep away too much of our date.

"Hungry?" he asks without me answering the previous question. He's got on a pair of flannel pants and no shirt.

I bite my bottom lip at how delectable he looks. But my body must sense sustenance nearby because my stomach rumbles. "What did you get?"

"A little bit of everything," he says, taking off the silver lids. There's a hamburger, pasta, fries, fish, quesadillas.

"Looks yummy." I get out of the bed to grab some clothes, but before I get to my suitcase, he grabs me and kisses my neck, his erection nudging against my ass.

"I want you again," he mumbles into my skin.

I circle around and fall to my knees, then I pull down the waistband of his pants, freeing his cock. I grip the base and run my tongue along the length, my eyes on his the entire time.

His hand falls to the back of my head and his eyes grow more heated as I open my mouth over the tip and swallow him down. "Fuck, Marla."

I've never liked the sound of my name more.

Chapter Eleven

Hank

It's late and the view out the window is only darkness. We sit on the couch in the hotel room with a tray of desserts in front of us. Marla picks up a piece of cheesecake, digs a fork in, and offers it to me. I open my mouth and swallow. She's so sexy and beautiful. I hate that a small amount of guilt niggles at my happiness because of Laurie.

"What are you thinking about?" She leans forward and presses her lips to mine. "You look upset."

"Nothing."

She tilts her head and raises her eyebrows.

I remain silent, not wanting to ruin this night by talking about my dead wife.

She places the cheesecake down on the table. "You can talk to me about her, you know."

From her expression, I'm sure she means it. "I'm so happy to be here with you."

She wiggles her feet under my ass and leans her back on the other side of the couch. "Me too. But?"

"A part of me feels like I'm doing something wrong."

She doesn't say anything, and her face shows no reaction either. I can't tell if I've completely insulted this woman I care about after sleeping with her for the first time or not.

"She died so suddenly, and the circumstances were tragic."

I shake my head. "We're not talking about this."

She gets up on her knees and scoots closer to me, taking my hands. "One thing I think went wrong with Jeff and me was that we were never really good friends." She looks at the ceiling then back at me. "We never talked. Sure, we discussed the kids or their schedules or his work, but we didn't really confide about much else with each other."

I squeeze her hands.

"It's what scares me about Jed. Jeff couldn't be vulnerable with me—he saw it as a sign of weakness. So when things went wrong with his business, he'd drown it in alcohol or, as I found out later, women. He never trusted me enough to come to me."

"Maybe he didn't want to burden you with it."

She shakes her head. "That wasn't it. I couldn't make him feel better because he didn't trust me to do it. We never had that mutual respect for one another. We weren't a team. Look at Jed. Do you think I'd raise my kids to act that way? And I know deep down that sweet little boy I used to know is in there. I practically raised Posey by myself because Jeff was at work so much by then."

I chuckle. That girl is well beyond her years.

"I'm not sure what's going to happen with us, but I don't want another relationship like that," she says. "Our pasts are our pasts. Do I feel a little threatened by Laurie? In all honesty, I do. But that's my problem and I'll discuss it with you if I ever feel like it might overwhelm me or affect what we have. But we're new, and if I'm your first relationship after Laurie, it's going to churn up some feelings. And I want to be the one to hold your hand while you sort through them."

I shake my head at her.

"What?"

I lean forward and wrap my hand around the back of her neck, pulling her into me for a kiss. "Just you. You're amazing."

She shakes her head as though she doesn't believe me. "Would you tell me what happened? Or is it too painful?" She leans back, takes my foot between her hands, and massages.

My chest constricts. I haven't had to do this in a long time. Everyone in our lives is more than aware of the tragedy that took my wife. "It was on the small lake about a quarter mile away from the house. Chevelle was five. She was going through this phase where she would follow Cade or the other boys everywhere. She was sure they were always doing fun things she was told she was too young to do. The boys had been out on the lake a week earlier, messing around. But the weather had gotten warmer."

I take a moment and start back up. "I don't know all the specifics because I had all the boys with me at football. I know that Chevelle had fallen asleep on the couch before the boys and I left, so I suspect she must've woke and went looking for them, not realizing they weren't home. I pulled up to the house just as Laurie was running toward the lake, screaming for Chevelle. I threw the truck into park and ran after her. By the time I got there, Laurie was standing on the ice in the center of the lake, Chevelle beside her. We looked at one another with a sigh of relief as she told Chevelle to slowly walk toward me."

She runs her hand up to my calf, and I fight the tears threatening to break free.

"It was this shared look like, 'man, we almost lost her.' I remember Laurie was in her pajamas, her hair in a ponytail. A smile was just about to form on her lips as Chevelle grew closer to me. Then it was like a movie. Laurie stepped forward and this loud crack echoed across the lake. The ice splintered like a cobweb. Her eyes widened and terror flashed in them right before the ice broke and she sank down."

I almost feel the chill of the air that day. The screams that I recognized as my own later on. The boys coming to the edge of the lake. Me yelling at them to take Chevelle and to call for help.

"Our neighbors heard the screams and came running. I jumped in the water, but it was so dark. I couldn't see anything, and the chunks of ice were too big."

Marla runs her smooth palms slowly over my skin as though she's soothing me. And it does help. A little.

"Eventually I felt my hand brush against something, and it was her. I got her out. At first I thought the same thing I had earlier—that we'd dodged a bullet. You know? I got us to the side of the lake and our neighbor returned with blankets. I remember her dropping them and saying she'd keep the kids busy. She must've seen what I didn't—Laurie's blue lips and still body. I wrapped her up while her husband tried to wrap blankets around me, but I think my adrenaline had kicked in. I started CPR. An ambulance came and took both of us, but she'd been trapped under the ice too long. She drowned."

I release a breath, finding Marla with a familiar expression on her face. The same one of empathy or sympathy I got for years afterward. I haven't actually relived that story in a while. For the first couple years after she passed, I would run through what happened every day. Try to figure out if there was some way I could've saved her, something I should've done differently.

"I'm sorry."

I nod, lips pressed together. "Thanks."

"I know my words don't mean anything. I can't imagine what it was like for you all."

"Chevelle was so young. She still has nightmares occasionally, although they've gotten far less now. I worry as she gets older about the guilt she might feel, but she was five. She didn't know any better. So many times I wondered, why wasn't it me? Laurie could handle the kids so much better."

"From what I've seen, you've done a great job."

"Thanks." I open my arms and she hugs me.

Her lips skate across my jaw. "Thank you for telling me."

I nod and kiss the top of her head. "I'm glad you forced it out of me."

She playfully hits me and we both chuckle, though it sounds a little sadder than normal.

A few minutes later, when we're still holding each other, I say, "Marla?"

She looks at me. "Yeah?"

"I like what you said. About being friends and trusting one another. Having a true partner. That's a relationship I'd like to be in."

She smiles and kisses my jaw, laying her head back on my chest.

I loved Laurie. We had a good solid marriage. When someone dies, you tend to remember only the good times and the good qualities of that person. Sure, I remember us fighting, but we had five kids. That's a given. But we had a good life together until it was ripped away.

Spending this time with Marla makes me remember how much I love being someone's other half. I want to share that with someone again. But it's way too soon for me to tell that to Marla.

Chapter Twelve

Marla

A week after our night at Glacier Point, we're walking hand in hand across the Sunrise Bay high school football field. After the night we shared together, it was like the flick of a light switch and we turned from budding relationship into a couple.

Although people have seen us around together, we mostly keep to one another's houses for the kids. The snow is falling, and I wanted to go somewhere we could see the entire sky. Of course, Hank suggested the football field with some joke about having sex on the fifty-yard line. I might've been game if I didn't fear my ass getting stuck to the icy field.

"Want to go make out under the bleachers?" he asks, eyebrows waggling.

"Can we talk?" I ask nervously.

"Sure." He stops and tugs my hand, leading me over to the bleachers.

We sit next to one another, our thighs touching.

God, this going to sound like I'm giving him some ultimatum, but I don't have a lot of choice. Our situation is complicated. "I don't really know how to bring this up—"

He puts his hand over mine on my thigh. "Just to be clear, if you're breaking up with me right now, I'm not cool being friends."

I laugh. Does he really have no idea I'm falling in love with him? "No. That's not it. I don't have the luxury of time at my age and circumstance, otherwise I probably wouldn't even be having this conversation with you right now. Not that I'm asking for some major commitment. But the kids all go to the same school and it's hard enough for them already, having had to start new. Especially since Jed is in his senior year. Kids can be cruel, and I just can't..." I stop. What am I doing? I sound as though I'm asking him for a marriage proposal after only dating for a couple of months.

"Go on," he says.

"Okay, I'm going to own this and if you don't feel the same, so be it, but I'm done taking the back seat when it comes to my life and what I want."

A wicked smile crosses his lips. "Do you want to have sex in the concession stand? I have a spare key." He starts to rise off the bleachers.

"Hank!" I shout, although the smile on my face says I get the joke.

"Sorry. Go ahead." He eases back down and urges me with his hand squeezing mine.

"I like you a lot, and although it hasn't been long, I see this working out between us, as crazy as that sounds." My stomach pitches at the thought that he may not feel the same. "I guess I'm telling you this because I need to know where you stand. If this relationship is a way to get back at your cousin—which I don't think it is, but I have to ask because for some reason, my head doesn't always hear my gut. But if we do this and it crashes and burns, my kids will feel the brunt of the fall and I can't have that and know I didn't directly ask. That I allowed it to just play out. I can't gamble with my kids' lives."

He stares out into the darkness of the field, only illuminated by the full moon above.

God, say something. Anything. Say I'm crazy.

"I don't gamble with my kids either. There are things that scare me with you." He pauses, and I hold my breath. "I'm terrified of this being harder than either of us imagine. Cade is beyond furious about us dating. Jed never looks too happy either. Posey made me promise when I showed up for our first date that I wouldn't hurt you."

Oh, my sweet girl.

"When we come out, this town is going to have a field day with the gossip." He looks at me. "If Jeff comes and asks for you back, what will you say?"

I shake my head. "That's over. One hundred percent. What if I don't live up to what you had with Laurie?"

His hand moves from covering mine to cupping my chin. "Don't ever think that. I'm not comparing what I had with Laurie to what we have, and neither should you. I guess what I'm saying is, there's a lot on the line. More than when we were in high school. But you've always been in here in some way. Even when we were just friends." He covers his heart with his free hand. "I don't play games or give one shit about Jeff. I want this, Marla, and I think the good that can come from us being together outweighs the struggles we're going to go through."

"So what does that mean?" I ask.

He leans forward, his lips millimeters from mine. "I'm all in."

"Really?" I whisper back.

"Somewhere in the middle of this, I… oh hell, I've fallen in love with you."

"Me too." I sound like a teenage girl who just scored her dream guy, but my heart sores and my body feels as though it could float away.

He crashes his lips to mine and his hand on my hip urges me up and over him so I'm straddling his hips. Our lips are frantic. His hands roam my body, falling to my ass, pushing me forward so I rock against his hard dick.

"God, I want you," he says, breaking the kiss for his lips to travel down my jaw. My head falls back and he casts open-mouthed kisses along the center of my neck. His hands roam up under the hem of my thick sweater. "You have no idea how many times I've beaten off to you in that cami."

I giggle, my hand falling down his stomach. I unbutton his pants, digging my hand down the front, past the elastic waistband of his boxers until I hold the weight of his length in my palm.

"Fuck." His teeth nip at my neck. "Sweater off now."

With the use of one of his hands and one of mine, we discard it, tossing it out of the way. Goose bumps break out across my skin, but Hank is enough to keep me warm. Or distracted at least.

As his breath is growling when I grip him tighter and he's bucking into my hand, a flashlight shines into Hank's eyes from below.

"What's going on here?"

I turn, catching sight of a police badge on the man's chest, and scramble to get off Hank's lap.

"It's like we're back in high school." Hank laughs as I

throw my sweater back on. He buttons himself back up and stands, making his way down to talk to the cop.

I'm mortified as the police officer asks the dreaded question, "What are you two doing here?"

I can't help but love the rush of excitement that comes from discovering this playful side of myself—even if it might get me in trouble.

Chapter Thirteen

Hank

Sunday morning, I decide it's a breakfast out morning for the Greene clan—mostly because I haven't gotten to the grocery store. We load up in my truck and head downtown to Two Brothers and an Egg. The local station is on the radio, talking about fishing weather and the type of fish that are biting. There's only ever local news and seventies music because the town voted and since most of our population are my parents' age or slightly younger, they went with the seventies.

The DJ, Chip, gets on the air and tells everyone about today's expected wind speeds and what bait they should use if they're headed out on the water. "And now I want to welcome a new segment I've been asked to add. It's called 'Locals Behaving Badly.'"

"What's this?" Cade turns up the volume.

So far today he hasn't given me a ton of hell, which is a nice change. Then again, he doesn't know about the cops finding me making out with Marla on the bleachers. Thank God I was able to talk us out of that one.

"An anonymous follower thought it might be fun to provide updates about any locals caught doing things they shouldn't. I think it'll bring some new life to this news station, and to that point, our first story is really juicy. If you have kids in the room, you might want to turn the volume down for a minute."

Cade laughs and turns it up louder.

"Your sister and brother are in the car," I warn him with a glare.

"Chevelle and Adam, cover your ears," he says.

I watch through the rearview mirror as they actually listen to him. I don't know whether to be happy or sad that they view him as an authority figure. It probably means I've been working too much.

"Cade, it's just gossip," I say.

"Shh..." His eyes are lit up with anticipation. It's a look I haven't seen since Jed showed up at his high school, so I glance one more time at the youngest Greenes to make sure their ears are covered.

"Everyone is aware that Marla Greene returned to town with her kids but no Jeff Greene in tow. Those of us who went to high school with her know about the brief moment senior year when we thought she was destined to be with another Greene from Sunrise Bay."

My hand goes for the dial, but Cade laughs, swiping my hand away. Since I'm stuck in a turn, it's either let it play out or side swipe a car.

"Well, get a load of this... last night, Marla and Hank were caught trying to relive some old memories on the high school football field. Things got hot and heavy and they were found making out in the bleachers. Who knows where things would've gone if the cop hadn't found Hank with his pants down?"

"Dad!" Fisher yells from the back seat.

I change the station, pissed off.

Cade throws himself back in the seat with so much force, Chevelle flinches. "My life is officially over." The smile on his face turns into a scowl.

I'm officially the worst dad ever.

"I don't get it. Why did Dad have his pants off?" Xavier asks.

"I can't even think about it," Fisher says, rubbing his eyes as if the visual of me with a woman will haunt him for eternity.

"Seriously? Are you trying to kill my entire social life?" Cade seethes.

I park along the curb outside Two Brothers and an Egg. "Let's just have breakfast and drop it."

Cade looks out the window. There's already a line forming outside the restaurant. "Hell. No."

"Watch it," I say.

"I'm not going in there so everyone can stare at us because you can't control yourself."

I run my hand down my face and turn around in the seat. "Listen." I remove Chevelle's hands from her ears. Adam removes his. "I want you all to understand that what's between Marla and I is serious, so you're going to hear things about us. Yes, we're dating but it's more than that. I'm in love with her. I understand that this is the first time any of you have seen me with a woman who isn't your mother. I know it might make you uncomfortable, but..."

Cade opens the door, slams it, and walks down the sidewalk.

I sigh.

Fisher joins him a second later. It doesn't take long for Xavier to tag along.

"Where are they going?" Chevelle asks.

"Let's just have some breakfast. Do you guys have any questions?"

Adam shrugs. "I like Marla."

I ruffle his hair. "I'm glad."

"Won't Mommy be mad?" Chevelle asks.

My heart petrifies and cracks, turning to ash.

"Mom is dead," Adam says matter-of-factly to his little sister.

I glare at Adam, and he shrugs like "What does she not understand?"

I put my hand on Chevelle's knee. "I think Mommy would want me to be happy, and spending time with Marla makes me happy."

"But..." Her bottom lip quivers.

God, this is a thousand times harder than I thought it would be.

"She's not coming back. You understand that, right?" Adam says to Chevelle.

Through the window, I spot Chip from the radio station walking by. Obviously the report we listened to was recorded earlier. I wonder how many times that thing is gonna be aired. He's busy shaking hands and laughing with some of the people in line. Laughing at my fucking expense.

"Just sit tight for a second," I tell my two youngest and grab the keys out of the ignition, stepping out of my truck.

Lucky for me, Chip is at the tail end of my truck. Hopefully what I'm about to do won't be witnessed by my kids.

"Chip!"

He turns around with a smirk as he nods in my direction, saying goodbye to the other guy who must see my expression isn't a good one because his eyes widen.

"Hey, Romeo," Chip says.

I cock my fist back and punch him clean across the face. "That's for playing with people's lives."

His hand flies to his jaw and he scrambles to get back on his feet. Not my best moment, especially since there are now faces plastered to the windows of Two Brothers and an Egg, but I'm not gonna let him think he can talk about me and hurt my kids that way. "Hey, man, I wasn't the one who wanted it."

"And who did?" I'm usually a cool-mannered guy. Not much upsets me, but I have five kids who will have to deal with the fallout from his report. What this will do to Marla and her reputation in town only makes it worse.

"It was your mom."

"What?"

He steps back as though he's afraid I'm going to hit him again, holding up his hands. "Her and that new friend of hers. They came to me this morning with the story. Thought it might break the ice for you two so you can stop hiding. And the station's ratings are down. I'm sorry, Hank."

The anger boiling inside me dissipates to a simmer. "I'm sorry, Chip." I wince at the bruise that's already forming. "Put some ice on that."

I climb back into my truck and start the engine.

"I thought we were eating breakfast?" Adam asks.

"Change of plans. We're going to Grandma's."

"Yay!" Chevelle yells.

Before I go, I shoot off two texts. The first is to Cade.

.   .   .

Me: You better watch your brothers. I'm going to Grandma's if you want to meet me there otherwise I'll see you at home.

The second text is harder to find words for.

Me: You might already know this, but we've been outed to the entire town by the local radio station. You might want to talk to your kids today. Don't worry, I'm handling the source it came from to make sure it doesn't happen again.

I toss my phone into the center console and head to my parents' house, which sits just outside of the downtown, up on a mountainside with a perfect view of the bay. I park in the circular drive and slam the truck door. Adam comes to my side, Chevelle skipping ahead of us up the pathway.

Using my key, I open the front door, but I stop in my tracks when I see boxes stacked everywhere.

"Is Grandma moving?" Adam asks.

I look down at him.

Chevelle skips into one room and right back out. "It's empty."

I shake my head. What the hell is going on?

Chapter Fourteen

"Fine. Date your cousin."
-Jed Greene

Marla

Hank: You might already know this, but we've been outed to the entire town by the local radio station. You might want to talk to your kids today. Don't worry, I'm handling the source it came from to make sure it doesn't happen again.

Me: I heard it this morning. Planning on a family breakfast discussion. Hope things are okay with you.

Hank doesn't get back to me, which I hope doesn't mean things are imploding on his end. Posey sidles up next to me at the table. I've allowed the kids to sleep in today, which is good because after the wonderful Chip Cooperton decided to out me and Hank to all of our hometown, I need the kids to hear about how serious our relationship is from me and not someone else. Especially since now everyone will be talking about it.

I kiss the top of her head. "Cereal?"

"Can you make pancakes?"

I smile at my usually too-mature eight-year-old who thankfully isn't acting like an adult this morning. "Why don't you help me?"

She sits up straighter. "Can I crack the eggs?"

I slide out of my chair and nod. "Yep."

"Yay!"

I decide to make a big breakfast. Hopefully full bellies will make up for the fact I'm going to break some harsh news to them this morning.

By the time the hash browns are done, Mandi comes downstairs in what has become all she wears these days— flannel pants and sweatshirts. She leans against me, and I hug her to my side, kissing her temple.

"How was last night?" she asks.

I nod. "It was fun. Thank you for asking."

She nods and grabs plates, setting them on the table. Nikki comes down minutes later and surprisingly doesn't argue with her sister over the fact that she's wearing Nikki's sweatshirt. Hopefully that's a good sign.

"Bacon?" Jed joins us ten minutes later and steals a piece from the paper plate.

"Can you get the milk and juice out of the fridge?" I ask.

"Sure thing."

"I'll get the cups," Nikki says.

I look at Posey, who is manning the pancake station with a spatula that looks bigger than her head, and smile. In the year and a half since the divorce, we've found our groove. Then I frown when I realize I'm about to throw a boulder in the middle of the road for us. For a moment, I ponder just letting us have this day, but I worry they'll hear my news from someone else.

Once we're sitting down to eat, we go around the table and play a game of Guess Who. You tell three facts about anyone from a celebrity to a sports figure to an everyday person we all know and see who guesses the right answer. Although Posey and I sometimes play, the older kids stopped being interested around the time of the divorce. I chalked it up to them growing older and too mature. So it's nice to enjoy the game with them again.

Jed finishes eating first, rising from the table and announcing he's going to meet some of the guys from the football team at the movie theater.

"Wait, Jed. Can you sit back down?"

He places his dish in the sink and he must hear something in my voice because his eyebrows draw down. He slowly returns to the table, folding himself back into the kitchen chair, eyes on me the entire time.

"What's wrong?" Nikki asks. She has every right to assume the worst. These family discussions only really happen when their lives are about to be upheaved.

"You're scaring me. Is it about Daddy?" Posey asks.

I shake my head.

"Are we moving again?" Mandi pipes up.

I shake my head again. The words are on the tip of my tongue, but they won't come out because I have no idea what will happen when they do. "We're staying in Sunrise Bay. Hopefully we'll be in our own house before Grandma and Grandpa return. Dad is fine in Arizona. I'm sure he'll make his weekly call tonight."

"Then what?" Jed asks.

Posey slides into the chair closest to her brother, and he puts his arm around her as though he's going to protect her.

The comforting move puts tears in my eyes because I haven't seen that side of Jed since we moved up here.

"As you all know, I've been seeing Hank Greene for a bit."

Nikki rolls her eyes. "We know, and I hope no one has seen you guys because he's kinda related to you."

I pat her hand. "He's not related to me. He's your dad's cousin, which makes him—"

"Our cousin once removed, but not Mom's," Posey says.

I point at her, assuming she's right. I don't know why I always find figuring it out so confusing.

"Still, he's related to us. It's weird," Mandi says.

All the children nod except for my sweet Posey.

I shake my head. "He's not related to *me*."

Own this, Marla. You are their mother and you deserve to be happy. This isn't the end of the world. A happy mother only sets a better example for her daughters.

"Anyway, I'm not young anymore, and I'm not interested in dating around and playing the field."

Jed releases a huge breath. "Thank God. So you're done with this dating thing? I mean, I don't really care if you date, but you chose the one guy in this town who has the same last name as us. It's creepy."

My head falls forward and I massage my temples.

"Jeez, Mom, I was ready to say I wanted to live with Dad," Nikki says.

My head whips in her direction. That's not even an option. No matter who I date, she's not living with him and his girlfriend. "Listen. Stop with all these comments. Hank is your dad's cousin, therefore I am not related to the man. If I had chosen to take back my maiden name after the divorce, he and I wouldn't even have the same last name. Can we please all agree on that?"

They nod, though hesitantly.

"I am only going to date Hank Greene. I love him and he loves me and we're going to explore a relationship with one another. What I'm telling you is that this is serious between us."

Jed groans.

Nikki's head falls to the table with a quiet bang.

Mandi's eyes widen.

Posey sits there beaming at me.

"I know you all have your concerns about this, but I didn't say we're getting married or anything like that. But I refuse to hide from you the fact I'm seeing someone. You're all old enough to understand why I might want some companionship in my life. It might work out or it might not, but Hank and I are grown-ups. We are the parents."

"So that's it? It's done? We don't have a say?" Jed asks, Nikki's head bobbing in agreement. I see they're going to be the hardest to win over.

"I understand that you've never seen me with a man who wasn't your father, so it will be hard for you. And I'm not suggesting you have to be happy *about* it, but I would like it if you were happy *for* me because Hank makes me happy."

"Did you two, like, really date in high school? Is this like one of those Hallmark movies where you always loved him, but you married Dad?" Nikki asks.

I almost laugh because it sounds like the rumors were already spreading about us even before the radio station report. "No. Hank and I were friends. That's all. I loved your father. When your dad and I split up I was really sad, as you probably know."

They all nod. Tears come to my eyes as I remember how I wanted to spare them from seeing how broken I was.

"I'm not sad now, but Hank..." How do I tell my kids he

gives me butterflies and stomach flips like when I was seventeen and I'd catch him smiling at me in the hallway? How I can't stop laughing and smiling when I'm around him? "Let's just say, I'm choosing happiness. And I understand that it's hard on you, but I'd really appreciate your support."

Posey crawls into my lap and puts her small arms around my neck in a tight hug. "I support you."

Nikki and Mandi reach across the table.

"We do too. I still think it's a Hallmark movie," Nikki says.

Jed sits there, and we all look at him. He sighs. "They're going to bust my balls about this at school even more now that you're official. Cade hates me. And..." He releases a deep breath. "Fine. Date your cousin."

"He's not her cousin!" all four of us girls scream, and we laugh together.

I grab Jed's hand and he squeezes mine, which hopefully is a sign he might not be ecstatic, but he'll deal with it. Everyone picks up dishes, assuming the family discussion is over.

"One more thing," I say. "I guess the radio station in town reported that Hank and I went on the date and..." I bite my lip. I cover Posey's ears and she squirms. "We were caught on the bleachers last night, kissing."

"Mom!" Nikki yells.

"Way to make it easy on us." Jed shakes his head and walks away.

I let go of Posey's ears and she looks around. "What did I miss? Come on. I can't be the only one who doesn't know."

"Mom kissed Hank and everyone in town knows," Mandi says.

"Mandi!"

She shrugs and walks away. "Believe me, she was gonna find out."

As the kitchen clears out, I sit at the table and sigh. I've got good kids. Hopefully this doesn't mess them up too much. But I can't shake the feeling that in the long run, seeing me pick myself back up out of the rubble and moving on with my life will be good for them.

I pick up my phone and see that Hank still hasn't texted me back.

ME: It's done. Jeez, who knew I could be so scared of my own kids?

NO RESPONSE.

ME: I'm thinking of you. Hope everything is okay.

Chapter Fifteen

Hank

"Mom!" I yell into the nearly empty house, reading all the names on the boxes. Some have storage written on them, others Hank, then one says Northern Lights.

My shoulders fall. Chevelle is skipping from room to room, telling me how they're all empty.

"Hank?" Mom comes from the kitchen and Chevelle runs up to her, hugging her. Chevelle is almost as tall as her grandma now.

"What's going on?" I ask.

She looks at her foyer with the rounded staircase along the wall and the chandelier she'd always brag about because she found it at a flea market. "What?" She looks at me with a blank expression.

"The boxes!"

"Oh." She pats Chevelle on her back and hugs Adam. "So tall." She kisses his cheek. "I'm moving."

"And you didn't think to tell me this?"

"I was going to tell you." She pushes Chevelle and Adam in front of her with her hand on their shoulders. "I have some cookies in the kitchen. Fresh and hot. Go."

They both almost knock the other one to the floor trying to get there first.

After they're out of earshot, she steps over to me. "I'm moving into Northern Lights Retirement Center. I don't want the grandkids to think it's because I'm old though."

I have no words.

Since I opt not to say anything, she continues. "I've had so much fun with Dori, and there isn't anything here for me. You don't need me anymore and the kids are getting so big. This house is all just memories of how old I've become. The stairs hurt my knees. It's too much house for one person. It was meant to be enjoyed by a family."

"But why didn't you tell me?"

She giggles. "You've had your hands full. Or maybe that's Marla."

I ignore her comment for the moment. "But Northern Lights is in Lake Starlight."

"You act like it's in the lower forty-eight. It's a twenty-minute drive." She moves into the family room, and sure enough, it's half packed, though the furniture's still there. "This is just too much space. It was too big of a house even when there were three of us, and now it's just me."

I stare at a picture of the land back when my dad bought it. He'd decided to leave Anchorage when Sunrise Bay was nothing but a fishing town. He owned the land for almost eight years, building the house bit by bit until he finished it. My mom says he was never around during her pregnancy, but it was worth it to bring me home from the hospital to this house.

"The kids still need you."

She pats my cheek. "And I'll be there whenever you want. I can still drive, you know. But you all have your own lives."

I guess she's right. The boys are older, and they don't want anything to do with me, let alone their grandma. It's only a few years before Adam and Chevelle are where they are now.

"Still, I could've helped you if you told me."

She waves me off. "Dori knew this moving company. They've been so good about being patient with me deciding what to keep and pack. I'll move a lot of stuff into a storage unit unless you want it."

I sit on the sofa and rest my forearms on my thighs. "Mom, how are you affording Northern Lights? It's expensive."

She sits next to me and places her hand on mine. "Your dad was always concerned with money. He worked so hard to give us the life he thought we deserved, and the day he passed that business down to you, he was so proud and happy. But I was in charge of the money, and my mom always taught me not to spend all your money when the sun is shining and there are no clouds in the sky."

"You mean save it for a rainy day?"

"No. I mean what I said. I'm not senile."

I chuckle. "Okay."

"There were years your dad didn't have enough work to fill his day, and there were others he couldn't keep up. You know how it is."

I nod, although my dad left me a pretty thriving business. Especially when he started doing work outside of Sunrise Bay. By the time I took it over, we were well in the black with four employees under our belt. Now I have six full-time and four part-time employees. Usually in the summer months, college students help me build decks, pergolas, and other outdoor projects for people to enjoy the few short months we have of great weather.

"So you have the money?"

She nods. "I have the money. You don't have to take care of me."

"And the house? Are you putting it up on the market?"

She hems and haws. "That depends on you."

"Me?" My forehead wrinkles. "I can't afford this place."

She moves my hand to her lap and covers our joined hands with her other one. This is her way of comforting me when she's going to bring up a topic I don't want to talk about. She did it when she told me about my dad's passing, and after Laurie died, I felt as if we were statues in this position.

"I know you and Laurie bought that house you're in now. It's the only one the kids know. And I don't blame you for wanting to stay there. This house does need remodeling, and most of the rooms haven't been used in years. But you're welcome to move in here. Your dad built it, so there's no mortgage."

I slide my hand out of hers and stand, walking to the back window. The pool hasn't been opened in years and is covered with leaves and dirt. The concrete surrounding it more gray than white. She's right about this place needing work, and that's probably on me because I slacked off on my responsibilities over the years. I should have helped her more.

"You're sure about moving?" I look back at her over my shoulder.

She nods. "You'll understand when you're as old as me. I need to be around people my own age." She walks over to me and we both stare out the window. "I know it needs some work, but you're a contractor." We laugh. "Just think about it. No need to answer right now. It's big enough for a large family though."

"Each kid would have their own room," I say.

"Or a few kids could share a room. It's not the end of the world. Plus two will be out of the house next year."

I look at her, confused by her math. Maybe she is going senile.

"Cade and Jed are going to college, no?"

"What are you talking about? Are you confusing Jed for Fisher?"

She rolls her eyes. "I listen to the radio too."

I point at her.

She must realize I know because she laughs and backs up, holding up her hands. "Come on. It's just a little push in the right direction."

"And three of my boys aren't talking to me right now because of it."

She waves me off. "So what? They'll get over it."

"Cade is already struggling with Marla and the kids returning. Your stunt didn't help."

"It's fun. People laugh. You and Marla don't have to hide now."

I inhale deeply, praying for patience. "I wasn't going to hide, but the kids don't want to hear about their dad and some woman making out in the bleachers."

She points at me. "Well then maybe you two should be more discreet."

I shake my head and push a hand through my hair. "Thanks for the tip. It wasn't your story to share, Mom."

She takes a rag lying on a box and wipes down the mantel, looking over her shoulder. "You're my business.

Your happiness is my utmost concern. Years from now, you'll be laughing about it."

"What are you, twelve? I think Dori's a bad influence on you."

She laughs, moving from the mantel to the end tables. "We have fun together."

"You never would've done something like this before you started hanging around her."

"This how you talk to your teenagers?" She continues to dust every wood surface in the room. "That's the great thing about friends. They pull out sides of you, you didn't know existed. Like Marla. She'll probably pull out things about you. Let's just hope it's not your penis in public again." She snickers.

My jaw drops. "Oh my God."

"Relax." She turns around to face me. "You're taking it too seriously."

"Because you put us in a bad position with the kids."

"Like I said, they'll get over it. They should want to see you happy, and I know that Marla makes you happy."

A smile tugs at the corner of my mouth when I think about her. She does make me happy, but we're in that beginning stage of a relationship when everything is roses. What if it doesn't last?

The front door opens and Xavier yells, "Grandma!"

"In here, sweetie," she says.

In walks Xavier, Cade, and Fisher. I knew they'd never walk all the way home. None of them look my way as they cross the room and hug their grandma hello.

"Cookies are in the kitchen," she says.

Xavier and Fisher walk out of the room first. Cade tries to move, but Mom grabs the sleeve of his jacket and tugs him back.

"You two are going to talk." She points at me and him, then at the couch. "Sit."

Cade might have a smart mouth with me, but not with his grandma, so he sits on the sofa without a word.

"I'm going to make sure they have chocolate milk." She leaves us alone.

I would usually say something about the kids having too much sugar and chocolate this early in the day, but skipped the restaurant and I don't have it in me right now anyway.

"Listen," I start because Cade would sit here silent forever if I let him. "I'm sorry about the radio thing. I know it puts you in a shitty position with your friends and the kids at school."

I get nothing in return. He stares out to the back of the house.

"And it was irresponsible for me to get caught on the high school grounds. I should've been more discreet. I apologize for those two things—although one is out of my control, you can blame your gr—" I stop, not wanting to make this about her.

Still he says nothing.

"I also understand your issues with Jed, but you're a good quarterback too. And whether or not you play quarterback doesn't matter in the whole scheme of your life."

His head whips in my direction. That got his attention. "How can you say that? You played, your cousin Jeff played, Grandpa played. And now I'll be the one who doesn't."

"You are playing, Cade, and what did me playing quarterback in high school get me? I took over my dad's business."

He sits up straighter and looks me in the eye for the first time in weeks. "Imagine another contractor came into this town and stole your clients and everyone bragged about how great he is compared to you."

My shoulders fall. I nod, understanding his point. "Gotcha. But all of that has nothing to do with Marla and me."

"Except that Jed is her son. And the kids are already saying shit about you two after you did the concession stand and went for pizza a couple of times after the games."

"And how does Jed handle it?"

"He makes jokes like he doesn't care. He calls me "cuz" in the hall."

I had a feeling Jed's personality was similar to his dad's, but I'm not sure if it's an act or whether it really doesn't bother him.

I look toward the kitchen and back at Cade. "After your mom died, I didn't think I would ever find another woman I could be happy with. Hell, I didn't even think I'd date. I was so concerned with you guys and getting you through the loss of your mom that it was the farthest thing from my mind. Marla and I never dated in high school, but we did become good friends and I did have feelings for her then. When she came back to town, it felt like there might be something there. I wanted to explore if that feeling was still there."

"And?"

"It is. I probably went about this the wrong way. But at the same time, I'm not apologizing for falling in love with an amazing woman. At some point, a parent has to live their own life, and if I thought she would be any kind of detriment to you guys, we wouldn't be together. Have you thought about Chevelle or Adam or even Xavier? They're young. Maybe having a woman in their lives would be good for them. Especially Chevelle."

"Are you going to marry her?"

I would never admit to him that I can see Marla and me married at some point. Not yet anyway. That would make me seem crazy. "We're not there yet. But I am in love with her."

He rolls his eyes and sighs, allowing his body to sink into the couch.

"You don't have to be okay with this, but you will treat Marla with respect when you're around her. You have a choice, Cade, to accept it or not, but I will not allow you to be cruel to her or her kids. Do you understand?"

He nods.

I stand to allow him to think about what he wants to do. I'm just about to leave the room when he calls out to me. I turn to face him.

"Can you at least just not kiss her and stuff in public?"

I chuckle. "I'll try not to."

He stands and breaks the distance with his head down. "I just miss Mom."

I put my arm around my oldest son. "Me too."

We walk into the kitchen. Just like when Laurie died, step by step we'll get to where we need to be. If I learned anything from losing my wife, it was that you can come back from almost anything.

Chapter Sixteen

Marla

Things are normalish in both Greene households since Chip decided to listen to two senior citizens about spreading gossip on the local radio station. Of course, a few jerks like to call us "kissing cousins" as a joke, but for the most part, people seem fine with Hank and me dating. We're out as a couple in public, holding hands, being affectionate, and having dates. It's a great feeling not to be hiding anymore. The younger Greenes are enjoying having other kids their own age to play with—with the exception of our two oldest boys.

I'm in the kitchen on a Friday afternoon, getting together some salad dressings. Two Brothers and an Egg offered to add them to the lunch menu. It's a small start, but a start all the same.

My phone rings and I press the speaker button, not bothering to look at who's calling. "Hello?"

"What the hell, Mar? You're dating our cousin?"

Jeff. I'm kind of surprised it's taken him this long to hear about it. Then again, he doesn't know anyone in Sunrise Bay. At least no one he keeps in touch with.

"Clarification. I'm dating *your* cousin."

"I always knew you had a thing for him." He disregards my comment because that's what he does. "I think I'm gonna come take Jed and bring him down here. His high school coach came to me the other night and said they need him for the finals. You know that team is going to state."

I try to rein in my temper. The last thing I want to do is make him angry. Through all our years of marriage, I learned to walk the tightrope. "And how does Melissa feel about this?"

"She's fine with it."

"Really? She's willing to give up all her Friday nights to go sit in a stadium filled with people and watch your son play football?"

"Yes. She likes the sport."

"I'll bet she does."

"This isn't about her anyway. Listen, I talked to my lawyer."

"You what?" I drop the oil and it spills all over the floor. My hands shake. Did he really think I would agree to this? He can't just yank his son around so he can live vicariously through him. "He's old enough to make his own decision about where he lives."

"And he did. I talked to him last night. How do you think I found out about you and your cousin?"

"Again, *your* cousin. He agreed?" I can't keep the hurt from my voice.

Jeff laughs. "Seriously, you should've stayed here in Arizona. Why you ran home like a little girl, I still don't understand. Moving Jed up there his senior year, of course he wasn't gonna be happy about it. Plus, if he wants to play in college, he needs to be at a top high school. Hate to break it to you, but Sunrise Bay isn't on that list. Just ask your cousin."

I clench my hands at his sly way of referring to Hank not continuing his football career after high school. I'm not even sure Jed wants to play in college. He's seemed happy the last couple weeks. Am I such a horrible mom that I don't even know my own son?

"I have to call you back." I click the phone off. My body sinks to the floor as I look at the oil spreading across the linoleum.

Am I really so stuck in my own bubble of happiness that I didn't realize my son wasn't happy? What kind of mother does that? My children's happiness means more than mine does.

A vehicle pulls up in the driveway. I hear a car door shut, then the front door of the house opens and shuts.

"Marla!" Hank calls.

I don't answer, but he finds me on the kitchen floor with my back against the wall.

"What happened?" He steps over me, grabbing paper towels to clean up the oil. "Are you hurt?" He drops the towels on the oil and crouches to my level. "Marla?"

"Jeff is going to take Jed back to Arizona, and apparently he wants to go."

"Who wants to go? Jed?"

I nod.

He sighs and his head falls back to look at the ceiling for a moment. "I'm here because we have something more immediate to handle."

I sit up straighter "What?"

"Just be calm, okay? It's about Cade and Jed."

My stomach sinks. "What happened?"

"They're in the principal's office for fighting."

My eyes close and my shoulders sink. Hank stands and holds out his hand to me. I take his offering and he pulls me up.

"Before we go." He holds me to his chest. "We are a united front. I know we're only dating, but I think I speak for both of us that this thing between us is only growing stronger. So when we go in there, we're a team."

"What if Jed goes back?" Unshed tears sting my eyes.

Hank shakes his head. "He won't, and if he does want to, we'll talk to him and change his mind. Don't let your mind spin out of control. We should've fixed this earlier with the boys, but we didn't. So let's go and clear this up with them now. Let them know they need to be a team too."

I grab my phone and my purse, agreeing with Hank. But my mind is filled with so many what-ifs, I have no memory of making it out of the house or into Hank's truck.

WE ARRIVE at the high school, where both of us know the way to the principal's office. In the waiting area, Cade is in one chair and Jed is in the one on the opposite side.

Principal Torres comes out of his office when he spots us and calls us all in. "Marla. Hank."

We both get a nod. Principal Torres was our classmate. Great. It's an extra layer of embarrassment that we have the delinquent sons.

Hank looks at Cade with a disapproving glare while Jed holds his usual cocky smirk. It's the one he uses in front of everyone who isn't family.

"These two got into it during lunch. They're both

refusing to tell me any specifics. I'm thinking of sitting them out of the game tonight."

"What?" Jed sits up straighter. Finally the smirk drops off his face.

Cade shrugs as though he couldn't care less.

"Whatever you think is necessary," Hank says.

"Seriously? My dad would've fought for us to play! Your dad's such a pussy," Jed yells.

Cade stands. "At least my dad can keep his dick in his pants."

Jed stands and they start toward one another.

"Say one more thing about my dad," Jed threatens.

Cade lets out an arrogant cackle that I'm surprised to hear. "I could list everything wrong with your dad and you. You think you're so cool and so popular. But you're a high school quarterback, and when high school is over, you'll be a has-been."

"Says the kid who lost his starting position," Jed fires back.

"Only because your lips are attached to Coach's ass. Look at the record, hotshot. We're not going to state. Almost every game you were quarterback, you lost."

"It wasn't my fault the receivers can't catch a damn throw."

Cade laughs. I step forward, but Hank stops me by putting his hand on my forearm. I look at him.

He leans in to say to me, "They have to get this out."

"Get a clue. Your dad is friends with Coach. They played together here," Cade says.

Oh my God. How did I not think of that until now? I look at Hank and he blinks in surprise.

"What are you saying?" Jed asks, but his cocky stance falters.

"You got my position because Coach is friends with your dad, and he called in a favor."

"No." Jed looks at me.

I shrug because I don't really know. I do remember Jeff playing with Coach Zeke, and I wouldn't put that kind of manipulation past Jeff.

"Before you got here, Coach was always bragging about his year and how they won state. How he and Jeff Greene are the reason they won."

Hank nods, apparently remembering it all. "I never thought he would... I mean... holy shit."

"What?" I ask him.

Hank shakes his head with a look to say, "I'll tell you later."

"You have no idea," Jed says. "If I wasn't better than you, then why does my old high school want me to play for them in the playoffs because they have a shot at state?"

Cade shrugs. "I don't care. Go back to Arizona. Make them lose for a change."

"Cade," Hank's tone is one of warning.

He turns to his dad, holding out his hands. "What do you want from me? He's taken everything away from me this year." Cade slides by Jed and walks out of the office.

Jed's eyes search me out. "Is it true?"

I shrug again. "I don't know."

But Jeff has always found ways of manipulating people to get what he wants.

"I trust you guys to handle this. They can play tonight, but detention all next week," Torres says. "I'll be talking to Coach Zeke as well."

"Thanks, Thor," Hank says, referring to him by his nickname.

This town is too small sometimes.

"Jed, let's go," I say to him, then tell Hank that I'll call him later.

Jed touches his cheek where a bruise is forming, and he walks out of the office ahead of me.

Hank grabs my hand and pulls me to his chest. "I'll check in with you later. But..." He looks over my shoulder. "You need to talk to Jeff. Zeke is sporting a new fishing boat. He was bragging about it at the beginning of the season."

I huff. "You're not serious?"

"I am." He bites his lip. "I'm sorry I didn't put it all together sooner."

"Don't be. It just means you're not a manipulating asshole." I kiss him quickly, and he squeezes my hip before releasing me.

Jed is outside in his truck when I approach. I signal for him to get out of the driver's side. He rolls his eyes but does it, and I climb into the driver's seat. I send Nikki a text to say she's in charge until I return home and there's oil on the floor in the kitchen and not to slip.

I drive Jed to his grandparents' house. Not my parents' house. Jeff's parents' old home. We park along the street and stare at the two-bedroom ranch that looks worse for wear.

"What is this?" Jed asks.

"This is where Grandma and Grandpa Greene lived."

"What?"

"This is where your dad grew up."

Jed sounds surprised when he says, "Grandma and Grandpa have money. Why would they live like this?"

"Your dad bought their house in Arizona. Your dad bought their cars. Your dad gives them an allowance every month. This is where they lived until your dad moved them to Arizona."

Jed's jaw hangs open. "Why didn't anyone tell us?"

"Your dad is ashamed. He always was. That's where his cockiness comes from. It's a protection mechanism. He's trying to act like someone he's not. I stood by for too long and allowed you to do the same. Jed, wearing a mask your entire life and hiding who you are isn't worth it. Did your dad pay Coach Zeke? I honestly don't know, but I can see it. It's your dad's way of making himself feel powerful and important, of making people do things he wants them to. And I'm sorry if you were one of his pawns. Maybe you weren't. He probably did it all for you."

"Bullshit. He did it for himself." He pounds his fist on the dash. "I've been an idiot. Playing week after week. Cade is right, I lost almost every game."

"But it wasn't all you. You guys are a team."

He's quiet for a few minutes and it's until I hear him sniffling that I glance over. "I knew, Mom."

"Knew that Dad paid off Coach Zeke?"

He shakes his head. "No. I knew Cade was better. It's why I asked his two best friends to work out with me." His head falls into his hands. "I'm just like him. I'm just like Dad. I manipulated the situation with the hopes that no one would notice." His back wracks with sobs.

Motherhood sucks sometimes.

I put my hand on his back and rub up and down, just like I did when he was a little boy. "You did what came naturally. But the good thing is, you're only seventeen. You can do the right thing and people will forgive you."

"Dad wants me to go back to Arizona," he says to his hands.

"He told me."

He picks up his head and looks at me, regret in his eyes. "He called last night. I told him about you and Hank."

I nod. "I know."

"I'm sorry. I was just so angry. I know it's not an excuse."

I squeeze his shoulder. "No, it's not, but you've been through a lot of change."

"I don't want to be like him," he says, looking me in the eye. "What if it's, like, engrained or genetic or something and I destroy my entire life like he did with his?"

I tilt my head, not understanding.

"Cheating on you. He ruined his life by cheating on you. I always thought maybe Dad could change and win you back, but I see how happy you are with Hank. So much happier than you ever were with Dad."

I look at him with a sad smile. "I am. I'm glad you notice." I take his head in my hands, willing him to really take in my words. "You choose who you are. You are the only one who can control you. You want to be a better person? You can. You want to be a better quarterback? You can. You want to be a better son?" He sighs, and I laugh. "You can."

"Thanks, Mom." He leans in and hugs me.

"That's why I'm here."

"Can I tell you something?" he says in my ear.

"Anything."

"I don't like playing quarterback."

I pull back and we laugh until we're unsure if our tears are from the crying or the laughter. Finally, I have my son back.

Chapter Seventeen

Hank

It's the last Friday night football game of the season. This could be Marla's last one, but with three boys coming up the ranks, I might as well pitch a tent and call the bleachers home. Marla and Posey are waiting for me at the field entrance, and I kiss Marla hello and pick up Posey.

"Let's stop at the concession. I need candy today," I say.

"Twinsies!" Posey agrees. "Third grade is for the birds."

Marla laughs, and I swing an arm around her back.

"I heard Cade is starting tonight?" Marla says.

"I heard that too."

She's giving me the look. The one she gives when she's apologizing. I can't wait until she trusts my reactions enough to never give me that look—I'm pretty sure it spawned from Jeff's reactions to things. But it will take time and I'm a patient man.

I drop Posey on the ground. "Go get whatever you want."

I position us so we can keep an eye on Posey and talk

privately. I tuck a section of hair that's fallen out of Marla's knit hat behind her ear. She looks as if she has something to say.

"What?" I ask.

"I just can't believe Jeff did it. I mean, who pays off a high school coach?"

I chuckle. "Jeff apparently. But unless you cut the check, I'm unsure why you're apologizing to me."

Her forehead falls to my chest. I place my finger under her chin and force her to look me in the eye.

"Cade missed this entire season."

"He played. Not as much as he wanted, but he wasn't going to be drafted. I think both the boys learned important lessons this year. Hopefully they'll develop a friendship that will stand a long time." I refrain from telling her I hope they find a brotherhood since with any luck, they'll be stepbrothers one day.

Looking out onto the field, I spot Cade with Coach Justin, going over a play. Zeke was let go this afternoon. I always liked Torres. But the surprise is that Jed is in their circle too.

"If they win this, they might get a spot. Sure, Greywall has to lose which..." My head moves side to side because they are a powerhouse. "But they could."

"All ready. They said they'll put it on your tab, Hank," Posey says.

"Posey, what do you have?" Mandi yells from the side of the fence where she's with Adam and a mixture of girls and guys huddled together.

"They only want me for my candy," she says before walking over.

A few minutes later, Chevelle and Posey emerge from the crowd with less candy than Posey started with. They climb the bleachers and sit down together, watching the cheerleaders.

"Come on. Let's go watch our boys play what might be their last game." I hold Marla's hand and she comes with me. "What did Jeff say?"

"He tried to deny it, but then said he didn't see the harm in what he did. Jed asked me to tell him that he wouldn't be moving to Arizona. Jeff said he was going to fight me, but I'm not worried. He won't."

"He's missing a lot," I say, my gaze bouncing over all of our kids.

We walk up the bleachers and sit down near Chevelle and Posey. Marla says, "He wouldn't appreciate it anyway."

The game starts and Cade runs out to quarterback with the first true smile I've seen on his face in a long time. Surprisingly, Jed jogs out right after him. Derek hikes the ball and Cade does what he does best, staying patient until he has a clearing. He throws it and Jed catches, running into the end zone for a touchdown.

The entire stadium goes crazy and the boys on the field chest bump. When Cade and Jed come face to face, there's a slight pause before they jump and bump chests, smiles on both their faces. Cade smacks the back of Jed's helmet, congratulating him on the catch, and they both get in position again.

"He wouldn't. The best things in life don't have monetary value, and he hasn't figured that out yet. Lucky for me." I kiss Marla as tears of happiness stream down her face.

Epilogue

Cade

Three years later

"**Y**ou do realize they'll be in their sixties when the kid graduates high school?" Jed laughs next to me as our Uber drives past the city limits sign of Sunrise Bay.

Anyone who knew us when we first met would be shocked to hear that we don't just attend the same college, we room together. Who would've known Jed is a pretty great guy? Still a little cocky at times, but I can be too. Our senior year, we scored the last spot in the playoffs but got eliminated right before state finals. As my dad and Marla always say, it's the journey, not the end result.

"They'll be showing up in walkers at his graduation." I slap the seat. "Our family can't get any weirder anyway."

"True story!"

There's a new baby in the Greene family. Rylan Greene. Only Hank and Marla Greene would decide to have a baby when there's light at the end of the tunnel of having nine kids out of the house. Though Jed and I have money on the fact that they didn't plan the pregnancy. No one really wants to think about how that happened, so we didn't ask.

I pull up to what was my grandparents' house and is now Dad and Marla's. They were quick to move in after their engagement that turned into an even quicker wedding. But Grandma Ethel is happy the house is in use. Jed and I both have dibs on it after they die (joking, obviously) because we had to put so much work into renovations being Dad's manual laborers.

The Uber parks on the hill where we can see the blue stork sign with Rylan's name, length, and weight. This kid's gonna be spoiled beyond belief.

"I'm starving," Jed says, getting out of the car and thanking our driver with a mumble.

"Thanks, man." I get out too, and we each retrieve our weekend bags from the trunk.

We walk into the house to find that it looks as if a baby store has exploded inside.

Jed picks up a box. "What the hell?"

"That's a breast pump, man."

His body shakes and he drops it back into the pile consisting of a swing, a stroller, two car seats, and a stack of laundry baskets.

Posey runs out of the family room, and her socks slide along until Jed grabs her and tickles her. "I'm too old for that." She squirms out of his grip but then attaches herself to his stomach. "I missed you guys."

She comes to me next. It's kind of cool having so many

siblings now, even if they are stepsiblings but also our second cousins.

"Come on. Rylan's awake," Posey says.

Jed looks back at me and we share the look to say, "Here we go."

We walk into the living room to find there's no baby. Marla's got a blanket over her shoulder. Dad's sleeping next to her. There's an entire playpen or something along the wall and a changing station next to it.

"A baby needs all this stuff?" I ask, looking around.

"Hey, Mom." Jed leans forward to kiss Marla on the cheek. "Whoa. Fuck."

Marla slaps his arm for swearing.

Jed shuts his eyes and turns away. "You're lucky I'm not blind now."

Dad stirs awake and blinks.

"I did it for you too. Hank is taking the real brunt of me breastfeeding. A new man has taken over his duties."

My head falls back and Jed looks as if he might lose it. "Seriously, keep that to yourself!"

Marla laughs, and Dad rises from the couch to hug us.

"Boys, you're old enough to understand I had to go cold turkey. It could be over a year."

"What's a little breastmilk," I say, and Jed picks up a stuffed bear and throws it at me.

It's not that I don't see Marla as a mother figure, but it doesn't gross me out the same way it does Jed.

"Good to see you guys getting along." Dad hugs both of us.

Jed seems oddly comfortable with the affection. But he keeps a lot in about his relationship with his dad. There's animosity there, but he never wants to talk about it.

"Where is everyone?" I ask.

"Here and there. No one is ever in this house at the same time, I swear."

Marla rolls her eyes. "They have lives."

We sit down while Jed heads to the fridge, grabs a bunch of containers, and fixes a plate.

Posey disappears upstairs.

"Hey, Dad, you mind if I borrow the truck?" I ask.

He nods and pulls the keys from his pocket, handing them to me, knowing where I'm going. It's usually my first stop before I come home, but with Jed with me, I couldn't.

"Family dinner tonight, okay?" he says.

"Yeah. I'll be a half hour tops."

Ten minutes later, I pull into Sunrise Bay Cemetery and wind down the path to my mom's burial plot. I park my dad's truck and walk up the short hill. Sometimes I'm still surprised to read her name on the stone.

"Hey, Mom," I say. "Just got in from school. Marla had the baby. It's a boy. They named him Rylan. He's healthy."

My eye catches sight of a blonde a few rows away. She looks familiar, but I can't really place her. She's openly crying on a new grave site filled with dirt and no plaque.

I shake my head. "So, anyway... school's good, and before you think about it, there's no one serious in my life." I laugh.

The girl lies down on the dirt and her head is turned. Is that Clara, Xavier's friend?

"Clara!" I yell, but the girl doesn't say anything or look my way. I turn my attention back to my mom. "It's amazing how things have changed. Jed's probably my closest friend now. Crazy, huh?"

The girl gets up, and yeah, it's totally Clara. Xavier and Clara have been friends since they were in diapers. The girl slept over at our house a million times and went everywhere with us.

"Grades are good. No worries there. No Dean's List or anything though. Sorry, Mom, hold up."

I jog over to Clara. The closer I get, the more positive I am she's Clara. "Clara! It's me, Cade. Xavier's brother. Are you okay?"

She looks me dead in the eye and scowls. The hairs on the back of my head rise, and my gut tells me something I can't decipher or put into words.

"My name isn't Clara." She walks down the hill and gets into a car before the tires squeal, announcing her exit.

The End

ALSO BY PIPER RAYNE

The Baileys

Lessons from a One-Night Stand

Advice from a Jilted Bride

Birth of a Baby Daddy

Operation Bailey Wedding (Novella)

Falling for My Brother's Best Friend

Demise of a Self-Centered Playboy

Confessions of a Naughty Nanny

Operation Bailey Babies (Novella)

Secrets of the World's Worst Matchmaker

Winning my Best Friend's Girl

Rules for Dating your Ex

Operation Bailey Birthday (Novella)

The Greene Family

My Twist of Fortune (Prequel)

My Beautiful Neighbor

My Almost Ex

My Vegas Groom

A Greene Family Summer Bash (Novella)

My Sister's Flirty Friend

My Unexpected Surprise

My Famous Frenemy

A Greene Family Vacation (Novella)

My Scorned Best Friend

My Fake Fiancé

My Brother's Forbidden Friend

A Greene Family Christmas (Novella)

Lake Starlight

The Problem with Second Chances

The Issue with Bad Boy Roommates

The Trouble with Runaway Brides

The Drawback of Single Dads

The Complication with the Best Man

Plain Daisy Ranch

One Last Summer

The One I Left Behind

The One I Stood Beside

The One I Didn't See Coming

Chasing Forever

Chasing Love

Chasing Home

Modern Love

Charmed by the Bartender

Hooked by the Boxer

Mad about the Banker

Single Dads Club

Real Deal

Dirty Talker

Sexy Beast

Hollywood Hearts

Mister Mom

Animal Attraction

Domestic Bliss

Bedroom Games

Cold as Ice

On Thin Ice

Break the Ice

Chicago Law

Smitten with the Best Man

Tempted by my Ex-Husband

Seduced by my Ex's Divorce Attorney

Blue Collar Brothers

Flirting with Fire

Crushing on the Cop

Engaged to the EMT

White Collar Brothers

Sexy Filthy Boss

Dirty Flirty Enemy

Wild Steamy Hook-up

The Rooftop Crew

My Bestie's Ex

A Royal Mistake

The Rival Roomies

Our Star-Crossed Kiss

The Do-Over

A Co-Workers Crush

Hockey Hotties

Countdown to a Kiss (Free Prequel)

My Lucky #13 (FREE)

The Trouble with #9

Faking it with #41

Tropical Hat Trick (Novella)

Sneaking around with #34

Second Shot with #76

Offside with #55

Kingsmen Football Stars

False Start (Free Prequel)

You Had Your Chance, Lee Burrows

You Can't Kiss the Nanny, Brady Banks

Over My Brother's Dead Body, Chase Andrews

Chicago Grizzlies

On the Defense (Free Prequel)

Something like Hate

Something like Lust

Something like Love

The Nest

Mr. Heartbreaker

Mr. Broody

Mr. Swoony

Mr. C (Title to be revealed)

Holiday Romances

Single and Ready to Jingle

Claus and Effect

Merry Kissmas

ABOUT THE AUTHOR

Piper Rayne is a USA Today Bestselling Author duo who write "heartwarming humor with a side of sizzle" about families, whether that be blood or found. They both have e-readers full of one-clickable books, they're married to husbands who drive them to drink, and they're both chauffeurs to their kids. Most of all, they love hot heroes and quirky heroines who make them laugh, and they hope you do, too!

* 9 7 9 8 8 8 7 1 4 1 7 5 6 *